THE

LONGBOURN

LETTERS

"I loved it! Brilliantly done, clever and witty — a real literary treat."

"A literary triumph!"

"A glorious epistolary novel that mixes laugh-out-loud hilariousness with serious social comment and often quite touching sentiment."

"A truly impressive debut. The language, the tone, the whole feel of the book are pure Longbourn. The letters' tale carries us beautifully through the years that follow *Pride and Prejudice*."

ROSE SERVITOVA

THE
LONGBOURN
LETTERS

THE CORRESPONDENCE BETWEEN
MR COLLINS *&* MR BENNET

First published in 2017 by
Wooster Publishing
Limerick
Ireland

Paperback	ISBN: 978 1 911013 754
eBook – mobi format	ISBN: 978 1 911013 761
eBook – ePub format	ISBN: 978 1 911013 778
CreateSpace paperback	ISBN: 978 1 911013 785

Produced by Kazoo Independent Publishing Services
222 Beech Park, Lucan, Co. Dublin
www.kazoopublishing.com

Kazoo Independent Publishing Services is not the publisher of this work. All rights and responsibilities pertaining to this work remain with Rose Servitova.

Kazoo offers independent authors a full range of publishing services. For further details visit www.kazoopublishing.com

Cover design by Andrew Brown
Printed in the EU

In memory of my granny, Nell.

I still feel you at my side.

People find meaning and redemption in the most unusual human connections.

KHALED HOSSEINI

Preface

In 1990, at the tender age of fifteen and while stretched out on my grandmother's chaise longue, I fell in love with Mr Darcy from Jane Austen's *Pride & Prejudice* and waited patiently for him to appear and wrestle with his conscience. Having since gathered some experience and knowledge of life and men, I realised that my true loves from the novel are, in fact, Mr Collins and Mr Bennet and I would now barely give Darcy a second glance.

Mr Collins, a comical, pompous anti-hero with as much self-awareness as a chamber pot, stands in total contrast to his detached, witty and socially-scoffing cousin, Mr Bennet. To me, they are two of Austen's greatest creations and their relationship, though rarely a visible one in *Pride & Prejudice*, was one that always made me laugh when I thought of it. A simple sentence from the book, in particular, triggered my telling of their tale – it is when Mr Bennet, greatly amused after reading one of Mr Collins's letters, says to Elizabeth, "I would not give up Mr Collins's correspondence for any consideration". It made me wonder what other experiences, observations and scrapes might these two men be sharing with each other through their letters.

In addition to that, I had wished to know what became of the Bennet and Collins families after the happy ending of

Pride & Prejudice. Tired of waiting for someone to channel Jane Austen in order to satisfy my curiosity, I decided to give these two eccentrics the opportunity to tell us all. When I started to write, however, I soon realised the game was up! These gentlemen had so much to say about their lives, while introducing me to a few new ridiculous characters (in addition to revealing more about Lady Catherine, Anne de Bourgh and Mary Bennet) that I simply handed them two quills and let them get on with it. My surprise on reading over their correspondence, when they finally finished, was that they not only brought out the hilarious, obscure and occasionally unlikeable in each other but that they had formed a closeness, which deepened and evolved over the seven years. It appeared at times to be kind, supportive and loving – emotions that men do not often admit in their friendships.

While the storyline of *Pride & Prejudice* ends in the second chapter of *The Longbourn Letters*, I have included a summary below, for those who may be only vaguely familiar with the great Jane Austen classic, as I feel it may add to their enjoyment of this book:

Mrs Bennet is greatly excited when news arrives that a wealthy young gentleman, Charles Bingley, has rented Netherfield Park. The Bennets of Longbourn have five unmarried daughters – Jane, Elizabeth, Mary, Kitty and Lydia – and Mrs Bennet wishes to see them married. Mr Bennet loves his daughters but is detached, cynical in his view of the world and content to let his wife fuss, once he is left to his library and books.

At a number of social occasions, Bingley's friend, Mr Darcy, who originally snubs Elizabeth Bennet, begins to find himself taken with her. Bingley is likewise attracted to her sister Jane. Darcy, who sees the Bennets' situation in life as much lower than his own, overcomes his attachment and convinces his friend to quit Netherfield by stating that Miss Bennet is not interested in him, and, with the help of Bingley's sisters, who are likewise against the match, keeps him in London.

Meanwhile, Mr Bennet's young cousin, Mr Collins, who stands to inherit Longbourn, visits the Bennet household. Mr Collins is pompous and wishes to wed one of the Bennet daughters. He soon makes a proposal of marriage to Elizabeth which she turns down, to the delight of her father and disapproval of her mother. Meanwhile, the Bennet girls have become friendly with militia officers stationed locally. Wickham, a handsome young soldier, confides in Elizabeth that Darcy cheated him out of an inheritance and reduced him to poverty.

All the Bennets are shocked to learn that Mr Collins has become engaged to Charlotte Lucas, of Lucas Lodge, Elizabeth's best friend. Charlotte acknowledges to Elizabeth that she must marry for security and this will be the best option for her. Mr Collins is triumphant after the recent blow of Elizabeth's refusal.

Some months after Charlotte's marriage, Elizabeth visits her at Hunsford Parsonage. Accompanying Mr Collins, they frequently visit Rosings Park, the home of Mr Collins's patron, Lady Catherine de Bourgh. Mr Darcy and his cousin, Colonel Fitzwilliam, her nephews, come to stay at Rosings where they meet Elizabeth regularly. One day, Darcy proposes to Elizabeth and in a rage, she refuses him. In her opinion he is arrogant and cruel and has ruined the lives of Wickham, Bingley and her sister, Jane. The following morning, Mr Darcy delivers a letter to Elizabeth justifying his reasons for interfering in Bingley's relationship with Jane. He also claims that Elizabeth was mistaken in Wickham, that he was deceitful and had attempted to elope with his sister Georgiana.

This letter causes Elizabeth to re-evaluate her former beliefs. When she returns home, she learns that the militia are leaving and will be stationed at Brighton. Her youngest sister, an attention-seeking flirt, is permitted to join them as a companion for the colonel's wife. Mr Bennet, wanting a quiet life, refuses to listen to Elizabeth's arguments against her going.

Lydia and Wickham run off together from Brighton. As they are unmarried, this brings disgrace on the Bennet family. The couple are eventually discovered and forced to marry, reinstating respectability for the Bennets. All are led to believe that it is their Uncle Gardiner who, through bribing Wickham, made this happen but Elizabeth later learns that her family's reputation was saved by Darcy.

Bingley returns to Netherfield and eventually proposes to Jane. While the family celebrates, Lady Catherine de Bourgh pays a visit to Longbourn. She confronts Elizabeth, stating that she has heard that her nephew is planning to marry her and wants her to promise that no such engagement will take place. Elizabeth refuses to make any such promise. Darcy, on learning of the conversation between his aunt and Elizabeth, tells her that his feelings have not changed and asks her to marry him. She accepts his proposal and they are wed.

Enjoy!

Rose Servitova
February 2017

Prologue

This book contains the contents of a collection of letters found at 'Longbourn', a dwelling dating from 1712, built on what was considered a moderate-sized estate in the Hertfordshire countryside, in the south east of England. The letters are correspondence between Mr Henry Bennet and his cousin Reverend Mr William Collins who resided at Hunsford Parsonage until his inheritance of the Longbourn estate on the death of Mr Bennet.

The letters, which were discovered on January 28th 2013 by its current owner while removing shelves from the library at Longbourn, were stored in a mahogany box measuring 30cm x 15.5cm x 15cm and wrapped in muslin cloth. The letters were divided into seven small packets, each representing a year of correspondence. Each pack had an outer wrapping of *The London Gazette* (it would appear, for the protection of the letters therein) and tied with string and an accompanying label, written in Mr William Collins's handwriting, naming the year and commencing: "The year in which …" with key events for that year listed thereon.

Examined by historians from the University of Hertfordshire, The Longbourn Letters were found to be in good condition, legible and undamaged, and subsequently their assessment and recording was approved prior to archiving at the University of Hertfordshire library.

The original mahogany box bears a copper plate with the following inscription:

> *Herein lies the correspondence between cousins, whose minds and souls forever dwelt on higher plains.*

> REV. MR WILLIAM COLLINS,
>
> LONGBOURN, 1817

> *"According to all that He promised; not one word has failed of all His good promise ..."*
>
> 1 KINGS 8:56

While not as extensive as the recently discovered Dutch Letters held at The Hague Museum for Communication, they do represent a reflection of the day-to-day concerns of the lower and upper gentry in Georgian England and, therefore, will be of particular interest to social historians and researchers specialising in this area of study.

The Longbourn Letters, none of which appear to be missing (according to their chronology and content), are written in the English language, by hand, in ink and quill and stamped with wax and seal as was common practice in the late eighteenth and early nineteenth centuries.

Anthony E. Loft
Head Librarian
University of Hertfordshire

22nd February 2017

1791 — The year in which an old quarrel between the Bennet and Collins families was resolved and the future Mrs Collins secured.

Hunsford,
near Westerham,
Kent.

15th October, 1791

Dear Sir,

The disagreement subsisting between yourself and my late honoured father always gave me much uneasiness, and since I have had the misfortune to lose him, I have frequently wished to heal the breach; but for some time I was kept back by my own doubts, fearing lest it might seem disrespectful to his memory for me to be on good terms with anyone with whom it had always pleased him to be at variance.

My mind, however, is now made up on the subject, for having received ordination at Easter, I have been so fortunate as to be distinguished by the patronage of the Right Honourable Lady Catherine de Bourgh, widow of Sir Lewis de Bourgh, whose bounty and beneficence has preferred me to the valuable rectory of this parish, where it shall be my earnest endeavour to demean myself with grateful respect towards her ladyship, and be ever ready to perform those rites and ceremonies which are instituted by the Church of England. As a clergyman, moreover, I feel it my duty to promote and establish the blessing of peace in all families within the reach of my influence; and on these grounds I flatter myself that my present overtures of good-will are highly commendable, and that the circumstance of my being next in the entail of Longbourn estate will be kindly overlooked on your side, and not lead you to reject the offered olive branch. I cannot be otherwise than concerned at being the means of injuring your amiable daughters, and beg leave to apologise for it, as well as to assure you of my readiness to make them every possible amends, but of this hereafter.

If you should have no objection to receiving me into your house, I propose myself the satisfaction of waiting on you and your family, Monday, November 18th, by four o'clock, and shall probably trespass on your hospitality till the Saturday se'nnight following, which I can do without any inconvenience, as Lady Catherine is far from objecting to my occasional absence on a Sunday, provided that some other clergyman is engaged to do the duty of the day.

I remain, dear sir, with respectful compliments to your lady and daughters, your well-wisher and friend,

William Collins

Longbourn,
near Meryton,
Hertfordshire.

30th October, 1791

Dear Sir,

Rest assured that the olive branch which you have graciously extended has been accepted by myself, Mrs Bennet and our five daughters. For addressing this most delicate of matters, I commend you most heartily.

You are very welcome to visit with us. Indeed, we will be waiting with impatience for the sound of your carriage as it approaches the house.

I fear, however, in comparison to the liveliness and grandeur of Rosings Park, you will find us quite dull. The ladies of the house are so often restless in the evening and I dare say will delight in any tales and intrigues you might relay of life beyond these walls and any passages and books which a learned man, such as yourself, would be kind enough to recite. My health requires that I retire to the quiet and solitude of the library but you shall find a ready and eager audience in my girls.

Indeed, I look forward to our meeting at last, that I may familiarise you with the nature of persons you will find hereabouts, that you will someday call 'neighbour'. You must be cautious on the roads, for example, for you never know who may be speeding along. This morning, on my way from Meryton, I met with Baroness Herbert's carriage, with her ladyship (all eighty years of her) up front, in cashmere shawl and bonnet, driving the horses on and her bloodhound sitting beside her, ears flapping in the wind. In the back of the carriage, propped up with cushions, was her idle driver, in full livery, whom she never permits to drive but insists accompanies her in the event that her horse should mount a ditch or a wheel come off.

Such will be the rich content of our conversations. Until November 18th, cousin, I bid you farewell.

Henry Bennet

Hunsford,
near Westerham,
Kent.

3rd December, 1791

Dear Sir,

I fear that I cannot adequately express my thankfulness to you and your family for the incomparable hospitality that was shown to me on my recent stay at Longbourn. I wish, therefore, to apologise in advance for any foolishness in my attempt at expressing my gratitude. My every need, from the repairing of my best woollen stockings to encouraging long walks for the benefit of my health, was tended to in a manner that astounded me and has been noted by myself and relayed to my patroness, Lady Catherine de Bourgh. She agrees that I was treated as would be fitting any clergyman with an association to Rosings.

I found my bed so comfortable and the furnishings of the sleeping compartment so above my expectations that I felt compelled to ask your housemaid whether I had been placed in the master's bedroom by mistake. The fireplace in the drawing room, I must confess, surprised me at first as a luxury not befitting a country gentleman of moderate means. When I realised, however, the frequency and standing of your many neighbours and visitors (Miss Caroline Bingley, Mrs Hurst, Misters Bingley and Darcy and Sir William and Lady Lucas) I duly saw the wisdom of such an expense. Your dining arrangements and the food served were both generous and informal, in a manner which reminded me of a supper I once enjoyed at Rosings when a whist party had been gathered.

I greatly appreciate your exemplary attention in ensuring I was ever occupied; in particular, your insistence that I spend as much time outdoors and in your garden as weather permitted, was particularly demonstrative of your kindness, knowing as you do my love of all things green. That you could witness my progress from your library window was especially touching and hastened my efforts to make some shape of your garden, which I found sadly lacking in attention. It does, however, hold much potential and will flourish in the future, under the steady eye of one who is confident in this arena.

But, dear cousin, to the crux of my letter. I have no doubt that my happiness is now known to one and all at Longbourn and I ask you, if I may be so forward, when next sitting down to dine, to raise a toast in honour of my betrothed, Miss Lucas. That I should have been so fortunate to obtain the affection and win the heart and hand of your young neighbour, following the initial but brief disappointment of being refused by your daughter Elizabeth, merely proves, yet again, that the Lord moves in mysterious ways. I am convinced that it was He who shepherded me away from my cousin into the welcoming bosom of Miss Lucas. And if there are now any regrets, which would be understandable, on the part of my fair cousin, I believe that her unselfish nature will not weep over spilled milk and she will truly wish, from the depths of her heart, that happiness for her dear friend that had once been momentarily offered to her good self.

With regards to my impending return to Longbourn, please do not think me sly or deceptive when I so readily agreed to your offer, though you did not know then of my motive, namely, my secret engagement to Miss Lucas. As with any young lover, I naturally wish to rush to the side of my bride-to-be and drink in the joy of this period of courtship. With her genteel society in mind, and with due attention to your own family, it is my intention to return to Longbourn on the evening of Monday fortnight, December 16th, and though it will be but a short stay of five days, it will enable me to fan the flames of my love and oversee the official practicalities which will secure me my wife by early January.

At our last meeting, you were so generous as to advise that I should not risk Lady Catherine's displeasure by making further stays from home and reassured me that you would not be offended if I could not make it to Longbourn for some time. I am gratified to announce, however, that her ladyship so approves my match, that she wishes to meet with my dear Charlotte at the earliest moment. She has, therefore, ordered me back to Longbourn, as soon as possible, that I may return to Hunsford, and indeed Rosings, with my fair bride. Not alone this, but she is coming here, to my humble abode, tomorrow morning in the company of Rosings Park's very own steward. She will scrutinise the parsonage and ensure that I am advised as to how to make any such alterations that would be acceptable to a young lady setting up residence therein. Such benevolence, interest and condescension from such a quarter, dear sir, to one who is merely a humble servant of God – have you ever witnessed the like? Am I not truly blessed in my patronage and is it any wonder that this must add greatly to my excitement and determination to conclude and ensure my matrimonial security with haste and at the earliest convenience? And will not my dear Charlotte feel equally in awe of that benefaction which lays ahead for her once she takes up the title of Mrs Collins?

I remain, dear sir, with respectful compliments to your lady and daughters, your friend and truly the happiest of men,

William Collins

Longbourn,
near Meryton,
Hertfordshire.

6th December, 1791

Dear Sir,

By all means come hither. We look forward to seeing you again though, no doubt, so much of your time will be taken up with your beloved Charlotte Lucas and we encourage it to be so. The period of courtship is so brief nowadays that one must enjoy every moment.

Please accept my heartiest of congratulations. I will ask Mrs Hill to have a large bowl of punch ready for the evening of your arrival, that we may toast to your health and happiness before you proceed, at speed, to Lucas Lodge (where you will only find very watered-down punch, as their housekeeper has learned of a temperance movement in London and is attempting to spread their wickedness here).

There is little use in hiding from you, sir, as you observed her discomposure prior to your departure, that Mrs Bennet encounters some difficulty in accepting your joyful news. Having witnessed the chalice of maternal satisfaction snatched from her lips by Lady Lucas, you may notice her displeasure again on your return, for she enjoys holding on to bad tidings and festering within.

The rest of us, however, are bearing up as best we can. We none of us would rob Charlotte Lucas or any of the Lucases one moment of pleasure in your company and selfishly wish it for ourselves. We shall content ourselves with our lot and remain philosophical as to the manner in which this affair has turned out. Perhaps you are correct when you state that the good Lord has had a hand in this matter and has shown great wisdom and mercy. "Give thanks to the Lord; for He is good." Psalm 136:1

Your cousin in affection and resignation,

Henry Bennet

1792 — The year in which a scandalous elopement occurs and a number of weddings take place. Mr Bennet undertakes the leisurely pursuit of gardening and Lady Catherine de Bourgh becomes enraged.

Lucas Lodge.

5th January, 1792

Dear Sir,

Please accept this note as confirmation that I have arrived safely at your neighbour's home in Lucas Lodge and can hardly believe that my wedding day is nigh. I must confess the journey was particularly cumbersome – a lady of excessive proportions sat next to me for the entire trip. I could hardly breathe and, on one occasion, fell through the coach door, which had a faulty latch. Fortunately for me we were stationary at the time, otherwise I could have been killed. She never apologised or attempted to assist me and though she was dressed finely, it was evident from her slouched demeanour and coarse manner of speaking that she was not high-born, most decidedly of low origin – 'place a peasant on a horse', as is the common saying!

May I take this opportunity to thank you for bearing my company a fortnight since on my last trip into Hertfordshire and I am quite ashamed when I think of how I frequently abandoned your comfortable home in favour of spending time with my dear Charlotte. The fire of my love leads me to act in such a reckless manner but, thankfully, two more days will see me at the altar.

Charlotte has mentioned to me her intention of requesting that my cousin Elizabeth join Sir William and Maria when they come to visit us in March, at what will then be 'our' humble abode, and I will add, it is my dearest wish also. That Charlotte will enjoy Elizabeth's company is my first cause for joy and that my cousin may see for herself, first hand, the benevolence which is bestowed on us at Rosings Park, I flatter myself, is my second. It will be an experience which she will no doubt wish to never erase from her memory, as I know how young ladies like to remember each and every detail, that they might relay it to all their admiring friends on their return home. And though I would never encourage envy, one cannot avoid humility, awe and reverence when encountering Rosings! But that we are in a position to offer it to her gives me great pride in my situation indeed, for she will be cast in amongst the most superior of society, such that the experience may quite overwhelm her. Perhaps, therefore, you should advise her in advance that it is quite common for persons on first entering Rosings and on being introduced to her ladyship to be struck dumb with the magnitude of the moment. Tell her to fear not, for Charlotte and I will both be present to cover up any ineptitude or incompetence on her part. As this is some months away still, let us not worry yet for there is still time for my cousin to calm herself and become familiar with, and relax into, the greatness of the occasion.

However, on more pressing and immediate matters, I regret that due to the severe weather and my preoccupation with final wedding arrangements, I shall not see you all until that happy occasion takes place in yonder church. I have just now discovered my wedding breeches are missing not one, but two buttons which would, most certainly, have led to a very embarrassing scene. I am also attempting to modify my footwear, for my dear Charlotte is, as you are aware, a tall lady. Hence the reason I write instead of visit and send my apologies, for I fear that you may misconstrue this neglect as malevolence on my part, therefore, I speed this note to you now by way of explanation, and wish you and all my fair relatives at Longbourn the happiest New Year wishes.

Your affectionate cousin,

William Collins

> *Postscript – I had not the opportunity to mention it before but I was greatly impressed with how you included Psalm 136:1 in your last correspondence. I cannot conceal that the absence of scripture and books on moral guidance from your library has long been a source of alarm to me, therefore, increasing my delight all the more.*

Lucas Lodge.

6th January, 1792

Dear Sir,

I fear I have not received any acknowledgement, as would be customary, that you read my note announcing my safe arrival at Lucas Lodge.

I am sending this urgent message with the boy today and a stern warning that he should not leave until he has secured a reply, for I know that you would be most anxious that I hear from you on the eve of my wedding day.

With respectful compliments to your lady and daughters.

William Collins

Longbourn.

6th January, 1792

Dear Sir,

Let me apologise, at once, for not formally welcoming you into Hertfordshire. As you have been in the county on several occasions already, I was quite unaware that it was necessary.

How unfortunate that you fell through the carriage door but, likewise, you were most fortunate that Baroness Herbert was not passing, at speed, at the time. She would have trampled on you for certain and not looked back. A rumour exists that she once drove her carriage through the lake at Netherfield when it was low, in order to follow the hunting dogs as they chased a fox.

I assure you, we look forward with great excitement to your wedding celebration on the morrow. Our Jane, as you know, is in town with her Uncle and Aunt Gardiner but the rest of our family shall be present to witness this auspicious occasion.

Regarding Psalm-writing, I am delighted that you do not find your cousins are entirely heathen in their ways. Rest assured that we do keep a hoard of religious literature in our library as fodder to the spiritual wants of my girls. Mary, in particular, relishes the stuff and I dare say you did not find a copy of *Fordyce's Sermons* as Kitty and Lydia enjoy it as bedtime reading, particularly in the summer when the light permits. It helps to clear their heads of soldiers.

But, sir, you have greater things on your mind!

Yours sincerely,

Henry Bennet

Hunsford,
near Westerham,
Kent.

18th March, 1792

Dear Sir,

I hope this letter finds you, and all at Longbourn, in the very best of health this mild March day. I must confess myself a little taken aback that you have not made the time to write to me and enquire after the safe arrival of your daughter, Elizabeth, into the glorious Kent countryside. I know my fair cousin has dispatched a letter last week with tidings of her arrival, howsoever this be the case, I still believe it appropriate to send a note to the host, in this instance, myself.

I know you to be a gentleman of excellent etiquette and therefore, I will assume that you are quite ill and have been so indisposed as to make the writing of a letter impossible and if this be the case, may I wish you a speedy recovery and recommend the therapeutic benefits of a very warm bath. Only last month I was doubled over on the pulpit one Sunday morning, suffering from acute stomach pains and excessive wind, yet I struggled on and delivered the shortest sermon of my career thus far, and thought frequently of our Lord on the cross to get me through my agony. Immediately after service, I was approached by Lady Catherine de Bourgh who demanded to know, in so concerned and abrupt a manner, as to what ailed me that I hovered so close to the ground. Whereupon hearing of my troubles, she ordered me home at once, to take a very warm bath. My recovery was miraculous *and instantaneous and the condition has not, I can assure you, to the great relief of myself and my dear Charlotte, made any reappearance since.*

Elizabeth has, no doubt, informed you of how her stay here is unfolding thus far and I shall only add that Rosings is featuring with great regularity and that my dear cousin is being brought forward and upward with marked attention from her ladyship. Indeed, I flatter myself that she is receiving such unreserved and scrupulous consideration due to her connection with myself, as my position of great standing in my patroness's home has not gone unobserved by her. The only criticism I have noticed thus far is Lady Catherine's disapproval that she, and her sisters, should be educated at home and without a governess. I immediately agreed with her ladyship and pointed to the lack of quality reading material that was to be found in the library at Longbourn (unless one wished to set off on an expedition to the Northwest Passage) and my grave concerns for their moral and intellectual guidance.

We are joined, next week, by Mr Darcy and his cousin, Colonel Fitzwilliam. What a lively party we shall be then! Mr Darcy, no doubt, wishes to pay his attentions to his cousin, Miss Anne de Bourgh, and what a magnificent match they will make. It is a wedding service I very much look forward to performing, as I expect the honour to lay at my door, and, I must confess, I have been putting aside eloquent passages from the Good Book which may be fitting for the sermon of such an auspicious occasion. There will be, as one can imagine, many great people from the most noble and prominent houses in the land present.

On another note, I am readying my rhubarb patch with vigour (the crowns I had taken from my late mother's patch) and, considering the quantity of buds which flourish on the gooseberry bush, I remain confident that I shall enjoy a great harvest this year. I believe I shall, confidently, enter a quantity into the Westerham Fair, my first time since taking up residence in this beautiful part of England. My enthusiasm has been dampened, however, as some local trickster did hide my hoe in one of the apple trees and it was most difficult to retrieve (in fact Charlotte, being taller, had success where I had none). He also spread some manure, which I had piled high near the rhubarb patch, just outside my back door that I might stand in it on exiting the house for my usual morning walk to Rosings (which, unfortunately, I did do). But I tell you, sir, there will be such a sermon from the pulpit this Sunday that the culprit will be very red-faced and shaken and it would not surprise me if he comes forward to confess his wrongdoing.

Finally, dear cousin, if ill-health makes you unfit to write in the future, I urge you to consider dictating your letters to one of your girls, if the subject matter be appropriate.

Yours sincerely,

William Collins

Longbourn,
near Meryton,
Hertfordshire.

17th April, 1792

Dear Sir,

Thank you for your concern regarding my health but I have never felt better. My physician confirms that I have the constitution of a man half my age. I would be sorely tempted to join the soldiers who are stationed at Meryton, but alas, they are leaving soon for Brighton. My youngest daughters (with the exception of Mary), and indeed my wife, are heartbroken, for to them they are but uniformed husbands-to-be and it breaks their hearts to see such a flock leave all at once, unhindered and unshackled. There is some talk of Lydia joining Colonel Foster and his wife. Would that they would take Mrs Bennet and Kitty too for I am sick of soldiers and those who talk of nothing but them.

I am most grateful to you, however, for your kind and generous care of my Elizabeth. I believe she leaves you tomorrow to join Jane in London and they shall have much to talk about, I am sure, considering your frequency at Rosings and its recent visitors, Mr Darcy and his cousin.

Sir William was so kind as to visit us immediately on his return from Hunsford to give us, in such minute detail (which I have not witnessed since his call to knighthood) an account of how he spent his every day. He spared no adjectives in his description of Rosings Park, the furniture he admired within and the herbaceous bushes he found without. Indeed, Mrs Bennet began to take notes so that she might relay all the particulars wherever she finds welcoming ears. I believe he may have been quite in awe of Lady Catherine, for he shrank before my eyes as he spoke about her. He also mentioned that your sermon, on the Sunday following the hoe-hiding and manure at the back door incident, was most effective. In fact, he did say that it moved the congregation to tears and then to fits of shaking … whether it was distress or laughter, he could not tell but he assured me, there was hardly a figure unmoved and unaffected by your words. Your sphere of influence, sir, is to be marvelled at.

Now, I must beg you, cousin, to sit down for I have such news as could weaken your constitution and return to you that ailment which so recently afflicted you at the pulpit. I have decided to follow your lead and enter my blackcurrants into the Meryton Fair which takes place in early September. I know I am a novice and have ne'er turned soil or pruned a bush (to the amusement of Mary who witnesses my attempts from her bench in the garden) but I find that I am strangely drawn to the pursuit of late, since your mentioning it, in fact, and am confident that my modest harvest will do very well indeed. Who knows what may come of this. I, perhaps, have chanced upon a new leisurely pursuit which will expand my lungs and increase my vigour. I thank you for setting such an example to your elderly cousin, for I surely would not have ventured forth into the botanical world with such abandon, had I not witnessed its soothing and favourably numbing effect on your good self.

Your humble cousin,

Henry Bennet

Hunsford,
near Westerham,
Kent.

13th August, 1792

My Dear Sir,

I feel myself called upon, by our relationship, and my situation in life, to condole with you on the grievous affliction you are now suffering under (Lydia's abandonment of her chastity in running away with the soldier, Mr Wickham) of which we were yesterday informed by a letter from Hertfordshire. Be assured, my dear sir, that Mrs Collins and myself sincerely sympathise with you and all your respectable family, in your present distress, which must be of the bitterest kind, because of proceeding from a cause which no time can remove.

No arguments shall be wanting on my part that can alleviate so severe a misfortune – or that may comfort you, under a circumstance that must be of all others most afflicting to a parent's mind. The death of your daughter would have been a blessing in comparison to this. And it is the more to be lamented because there is reason to suppose, as my dear Charlotte informs me, that this licentiousness of behaviour in your daughter has proceeded from a faulty degree of indulgence; though, at the same time, for the consolation of yourself and Mrs Bennet, I am inclined to think that her own disposition must be naturally bad, or she could not be guilty of such an enormity, at so early an age.

Howsoever that may be, you are grievously to be pitied; in which opinion I am not only joined by Mrs Collins, but likewise by Lady Catherine and her daughter, to whom I have related the affair. They agree with me in apprehending that this false step in one daughter will be injurious to the fortunes of all the others; for who, as Lady Catherine herself condescendingly says, will connect themselves with such a family? And this consideration leads me moreover to reflect, with augmented satisfaction, on a certain event of last November; for had it been otherwise, I must have been involved in all your sorrow and disgrace. Let me advise you then, my dear sir, to console yourself as much as possible, to throw off your unworthy child from your affection for ever, and leave her to reap the fruits of her own heinous offence.

I am, sir, your affectionate but aggrieved cousin,

William Collins

Longbourn,
near Meryton,
Hertfordshire.

4th September, 1792

Dear Sir,

No doubt, by now, the talkative and well-meaning Lucases will have informed you that Lydia is married to Wickham. I must confess I am not happy but it is done and done for the best. And while I must appreciate all your advice and warnings on the matter, we must bear this situation as best we can. Would he were sent to the East Indies for, I must confess, I cannot bear the sight of him.

My wife, and even Kitty, appear pleased with this patched-up marriage. Jane, Elizabeth and Mary take a graver opinion on the matter, as do I. We are indebted to the Gardiners beyond words. It is a subject I cannot dwell on for long. Please, for my sake, let not us speak often on the subject.

Your cousin,

Henry Bennet

Hunsford,
near Westerham,
Kent.

2nd October, 1792

Dear Sir,

I find, indeed, I have so much to say and know not where to begin. Yesterday, we received a letter from Lady Lucas informing us of the recent engagement of my dear cousin, Jane, to the very worthy Mr Bingley of Netherfield Hall. On this piece of news, may I offer you and all the Bennet family my deepest and sincerest congratulations. While I recall that we had all once anticipated a happy ending in that quarter, it was my understanding that all hopes had been extinguished and to learn that such an elevation should occur so close on the heels of the disgraceful marriage of my youngest cousin, Lydia, who will now become sister-in-law of the distinguished Bingley, is quite remarkable indeed. Such was my bewilderment that I enquired of Mrs Collins as to whether the gentleman was aware of the scandal, to which she assured me that it was commonly known and spoken about in Meryton circles. Having met Mr Bingley myself and finding that he was sound of mind, I must assume that he was captivated by my cousin's charms, for he certainly did not marry for the very acceptable motives of status, wealth or connections. Howsoever that may be, it is a most wonderful advancement for all at Longbourn and is to be broadcast abroad, where it will be of use to all the Bennet family, including my good self, who may also benefit, at some future date, from so dignified a connection.

Having thus offered you the sincere congratulations of Mrs Collins and myself on this happy event, let me now add a short hint on the subject of another; for which we have been advertised by the same authority. Your daughter Elizabeth, it is presumed, will not long bear the name of Bennet, after her elder sister has resigned it, and the chosen partner of her fate may be reasonably looked up to as one of the illustrious personages in this land. This gentleman is blessed, in a peculiar way, with everything the heart of mortal can most desire – splendid property, noble kindred and extensive patronage. Yet, in spite of all these temptations, let me warn my cousin Elizabeth, and yourself, of what evils you may incur by a precipitate closure with this gentleman's proposals, which, of course, you will be inclined to take immediate advantage of.

My motive for cautioning you is as follows: we have reason to imagine that his aunt, Lady Catherine de Bourgh, does not look on the match with a favourable eye. After mentioning the likelihood of this marriage to her ladyship last night, she immediately, with her usual condescension, expressed what she felt on the occasion; when it became apparent, that on the score of some family objections as regards my cousin, she would never give her consent to what she termed so disgraceful a match. I thought it my duty to give the speediest intelligence of this to my cousin, that she and her noble admirer might be aware of what they are about, and not run hastily into a marriage which has not been properly sanctioned.

I am truly rejoiced that my cousin Lydia's sad business has been so well hushed up, and am only concerned that their living together before the marriage took place should be so generally known. I must not, however, neglect the duties of my station, or refrain from declaring my amazement, at hearing that you received the young couple into your house as soon as they were married. It was an encouragement of vice; and had I been the rector of Longbourn, I should very strenuously have opposed it. You ought certainly to forgive them, as a Christian, but never to admit them in your sight, or allow their names to be mentioned in your hearing.

By now, you will have been informed by Elizabeth, who received the delightful tidings from Mrs Collins in a letter last week, that we are to be blessed with company in the coming months. My dear Charlotte is in great health and is wonderfully content with her situation.

My blessings, indeed, are many in this past twelvemonth and I give thanks to Him who has brought them to me.

I am, dear sir, your affectionate and fortunate cousin,

William Collins

Longbourn,
near Meryton,
Hertfordshire.

7th October, 1792

Dear Sir,

I must trouble you once more for congratulations. Elizabeth will soon be the wife of Mr Darcy. Console Lady Catherine as well as you can. But, if I were you, I would stand by the nephew; he has more to give.

Yours sincerely,

Henry Bennet

Postscript: I almost forgot, sir, please make haste with still more congratulations! I received first prize for my blackcurrants at the Meryton Fair last month. The judge, Mrs Hill's first cousin, said they were as good as any he has seen and incidentally made enquiries after my sow, whom he has been trying to purchase from me for many years.

Lucas Lodge.

11th October, 1792

My Dear Sir,

We have just now arrived at Lucas Lodge and wish to let you know of our unexpected arrival into the Hertfordshire countryside and your neighbourhood. Charlotte, in her condition, was eager to spend time with her family, while her health permits it, but, in truth, we are moved more speedily hither due to a matter of great concern to me.

Lady Catherine was rendered so outraged by the news of her nephew's engagement and let loose all her disappointment and fury, that much of it fell on my own head. She stated that my being Elizabeth's cousin, and Charlotte her childhood friend, were responsible for throwing the lovers together and, indeed, almost conspiring against her. In such a state of trepidation, we felt it safest to remove ourselves immediately to Lucas Lodge to take cover and wait for the worst of the storm to pass, though I must confess that it may take some time. I should never wish to witness her ladyship in such a distressed state again and pray that it shall not happen for the remainder of my residence at Hunsford.

I can only wonder whether her deep disappointment perhaps stemmed from not soon calling Darcy her own son, adding vinegar to the wound, for it was certain in her mind that fate would have it so. Indeed, I too am bitterly disappointed, for my vision of their wedding ceremony is crushed and there is no occasion now fitting my great passages. I shall bear it as best I can but I must confess I am perplexed that you did not heed my warning and part the lovers until a more convenient route be found. One wonders how he could be thus tempted to act in such a rash and unguided manner when he could have had Rosings in addition to Pemberley. I will, however, put aside my displeasure to add that I sincerely wish them well and assure you that, although it would be impossible for Lady Catherine to degrade herself by attending the wedding ceremony, both Charlotte and I would be flattered to be present. I believe I heard from the servants that not one, but two, pineapples have been ordered for the celebrations of this momentous occasion.

We encountered Baroness Herbert, her dog and carriage on the final stretch of our journey. Indeed she does move at alarming speed, displaying a wildness of character quite unbefitting a member of the aristocracy.

We will no doubt, sir, be delighted to see you within the next day or two.

With compliments to your wife and daughters,

William Collins

> Postscript: I am all astonishment with regards your prize-winning blackcurrants for when I first visited Longbourn last year, I shook my head with regret that the bush was in such a sorry state. I will not tell you, sir, that it was dead but it was certainly not alive. Your lettuce, which I momentarily mistook for cabbage, existed for the sole purpose of feeding the local population of rabbits and slugs. That the blackcurrant bush not only survived but went on to win first prize with its crop is a miracle, cousin, of biblical

proportions. I myself have enjoyed some little success at the Westerham Fair, third prize in the categories in which I entered, but as the first and second prizes were all won by Lady Catherine de Bourgh, I was deeply humbled and delighted to witness my name listed next to hers in the winners' logbook. In her current fury, however, all that is forgot.

Longbourn.

11th October, 1792

My Dear Sir,

I congratulate you, for you must be delighted. Elizabeth's impending marriage to Darcy makes you practically a nephew-in-law of Lady Catherine in all but name. Little did you think when you were casting yourself at her feet as a humble servant that you would one day look her in the eye as an equal and relative. I hope in time, when her fury takes a turn for the better, that she will relish, nay enjoy, the connection as much as we do. Fear not, your wonderful 'passages' will get a day out, at some future time. Keep them safe, sir, for you never know when your eloquent passages will be in great demand amongst the upper gentry of this fair land.

May I caution you, sir, not to trouble yourself with rushing to our sides on this visit. We know that you will be tending to the needs of your wife during this delicate time of expectancy and we would not have it on our consciences if she should need you at Lucas Lodge while you were entertaining us. Yours is a generous spirit and one we must take care not to take advantage of. If we see you within the week, we will consider ourselves most fortunate.

Another reason which would have me delay the pleasure of your company is that you would find us not quite ourselves as wedding preparations have taken over our lives, minds and purses. The weddings will be joined – Elizabeth and Darcy, Jane and Bingley. The date will soon be fixed and if you hold tight at Lucas Lodge, you most probably will be in attendance, for these lovers have no patience.

As you can imagine, Mrs Bennet has already made her way to the draper in Meryton for the sole purpose of returning to inform me that there is nothing therein fit for the clothing of one who will be soon the mother-in-law of both gentlemen. She must, she declares, absolutely must, visit the best warehouses in London in the company of her sister-in-law, Mrs Gardiner. I encourage it, and choose to forget the cost, for the few days of peace it will afford me. The older I get, it seems, the greater value I put on my time rather than my money. Mrs Bennet will take our daughters with her and so I will once again be free to roam my house without interruption and, temporarily at least, become the head of the house once more. Only last week, while searching for an old map of the West Indies, I entered the back room, wherein the lady of the house occasionally retires when she has one of her headaches, to discover I had not set foot in it for over a year and it had new wallpaper, a bureau and armchair which I had never seen in the course of my life. A veritable stranger, I have become, in my own home!

I will send for you to join me for dinner on one of these quiet evenings, when I have the house to myself and we can do as we please without offence to any other. It will also give me the opportunity to show you the first prize ribbon which my blackcurrants won for me and we can marvel together at this miraculous happening.

Your cousin,

Henry Bennet

Hunsford,
near Westerham,
Kent.

13ᵗʰ December, 1792

Dear Sir,

May I sincerely apologise in advance for the brevity of my Christmas greetings (and gratitude for your kindness to us on our last visit to Hertfordshire). I sincerely hope you will not be affronted by such communicative neglect for I find I am flustered and preoccupied this weather with an increase in religious services and fussing over my dear Mrs Collins. Sir, I do not know how you undertook this anxiety on five separate occasions.

Though we must mention it in a whisper, and not at all at Rosings, both Charlotte and I were delighted to witness the marriages, last month, of my dear cousins, Jane and Elizabeth. I may even be so bold as to add that though the weddings were most probably frowned upon in some quarters, there was such grandeur and excellent taste on display at the reception in Netherfield Hall that one need not hang one's head in shame to be associated with the event. In fact, Charlotte and I were just marvelling at how our social standing is ever spiralling upwards.

I would like to take this opportunity to wish you and all your charming family the most peaceful Christmas and New Year. As you know, we will be staying at home here in Hunsford this year, with the occasional visit to Rosings Park, as is our duty and privilege, if we are permitted (for Lady

Catherine remains cold). We expect, with God's good grace, to be joined by Sir William and Lady Lucas in late February, to be present with us on welcoming our new addition, and their first grandchild, into the world.

Please accept the warmth and good wishes of Mrs Collins and myself.

Your affectionate cousin,

William Collins

Longbourn,
near Meryton,
Hertfordshire.

19th December, 1792

Dear Sir,

May I take this opportunity to wish you and Mrs Collins and indeed all in Rosings Park the most wonderful of Christmases. I find myself at home alone this evening as the rest of the family are away at the annual Meryton Christmas Ball. Anxiety that Kitty is not yet married preys terribly on Mrs Bennet's nerves yet she appears to hold out not a jot of hope for Mary, nor does Mary, for that matter. I, alone, cling to the belief that some ruffian or other will be kicking in my library door someday requesting her hand (who is good enough, I would wonder?). The lady of the house, however, tells me not to be ridiculous, that no one will come for Mary, when the truth is, that she herself does not want to be left without a companion – for who will hold her smelling salts and fluff her pillow, if not Mary?

And so I find myself in my library with a bottle of port which the good Reverend Green gave me by way of payment for a goose. Did I mention to you that he walks an imaginary dog, our Reverend Green? No one has had the heart to tell him that Spot has been dead these twelve years. He even believes that Spot has sired my current litter of pups so, as a kindly gesture, I offered him any one of his choosing, believing the company of a real animal might be of benefit to him, but he refused, stating most firmly that he cannot be responsible for all that Spot begets.

I must confess myself more than a little merry, this fine winter evening. It is a very good port, I must say, I have not had one as good in many years but then, the goose was also good, and it makes one think of the complicated way in which geese are plucked and port is made and how we trade one good thing for another … amazing people, the Portuguese, when one thinks about them … setting sail there one day and finding the Americas and what not. Marvellous people. I met a man from Lisbon once back in my youth when I was staying with an aunt in Bath. She was an aunt from my mother's lineage so would not be related to your good self but you may have heard me mention her on occasion, a Mrs Stern (in nature as well as name). She was a sizeable lady. I once overheard a maid say she was obliged to throw Gowland's lotion on her mistress from a distance for she 'was as wide as she was tall' and could not get within several feet of her person. But, yes, I remember meeting a man from Lisbon at the Assembly Rooms when forced to go there and indeed, I struck up conversation with this man from Lisbon or is it Lisboa they call it? We spoke about coffee in fact; he told me some very interesting things about coffee and that the first coffee house was in Damascus, so you see it was not only Saul, from the Good Book, on the side of the road that made Damascus famous. Now that I consider it, this gentleman was, in all likelihood, from Madrid, howsoever the case, we spoke a good hour about coffee beans. Fascinating subject! If the coffee bean could talk of its travels, what stories it could tell!

And a very happy Christmas to you and your entire household, dear cousin. I must confess, I would not give up our correspondence for all the geese in the land, or for all the port either, for that matter, although the sacrifice be greater. Since we have become acquainted through the mending of an old dispute – and I must commend you again for your diplomatic extending of olive branches – I must say the relationship has enriched my life. Your tales and intrigues from life in Kent are, my favourite source of entertainment and I feel all the benefits of the connection without the need to be present myself, for such is your eloquence and gift with words that I have the impression that I am there, witnessing for myself, the scenes as they unfold. How grateful your congregation must be and how mesmerised they must appear upon your utterances and sermons for such is your way with words. It is a gift from on High. And it is not you, sir, who is fortunate in the connection to Rosings, but Lady Catherine who is the fortunate one, and I dare say she knows it too for she keeps a tight rein on your comings and goings.

I too am fortunate, indeed, to have a person of your calibre and disposition whom I can call 'friend'. Which is more than I can say for those frivolous gatherings at assembly rooms and balls – such tedious conversation to be had with cantankerous farmers and gouty gentlemen. And as for the ladies! If you had seen the satin, sir, which exited this house this very evening, in such a flap and in such vast quantities, as could have put sails on Admiral Nelson's entire fleet, you would have been most alarmed! Give me my library, cousin, a glass or two or four of port and Edward Gibbons *Decline and Fall of the Roman Empire* any day or night.

And so we prepare for Christmas or, in truth, we leave it in the very capable hands of Mrs Hill, and admire the smells coming from the kitchen, from afar. Ah, Christmas, a time when the weather gives us permission to stay at home and mind our own business!

I will bid you farewell now, cousin, but to say do not fret over the offspring which will soon be born. It is a blessing and by the time you have moved onto your fifth, you will be well accustomed to it. Let me finish by wishing yourself, Mrs Collins and all at Hunsford and Rosings, the most wonderful Christmas and New Year, if I have not done so already!

Your affectionate cousin,

Henry Bennet

1793 — The year in which the Collins lineage is assured, the Bennet family visit Rosings and Miss Catherine Bennet catches the eye of a gentleman friend.

Hunsford,
near Westerham,
Kent.

14th February, 1793

Dear Sir,

I am deeply humbled by your last letter which was full of praise and appreciation of my good self and, though I be the most humble of men, I felt it keenly. It was the good Lord, himself, who saw fit to drive me to the mending of a breach between our two families; "in Christ God was reconciling the world to himself, not counting their trespasses against them, and entrusting to us the message of reconciliation." 2 Corinthians 5:19.

I will make it of the greatest importance and urgency to include, when next visiting Hertfordshire, several journals of my sermons, for I keep them all. Had I known that they would mean so much to you, I would not have deprived you of them this long. We may retire to your library, of an evening, and I would be very happy to read from them, that we should both enjoy them at our leisure, for I do love to read back over my elegant turns of phrase and be reminded of how the Holy Spirit moves through me.

And now onto our most wonderful news! The good Lord is smiling down on us all here at Hunsford as we welcomed young Thomas Lewis Henry Collins into the family late last Tuesday evening. My dear Charlotte is well and strong and dotes on the boy.

I myself am suffering from a slight sprain to my wrist

which makes writing this letter excessively painful but I shall proceed regardless. It was a most unfortunate and poorly timed occurrence. I became aware that as Thomas's arrival approached, my dear Charlotte found my assistance and company irksome and I was in such a fluster that I slipped on the last three steps of our main stairwell, going backwards before flying forwards, head first into the front door. Fortunately for me, it was partially open, so instead of receiving the full impact of injury, I lunged through the door and slid along the gravel. It was most unfortunate, however, that Miss Anne de Bourgh, accompanied by Mrs Jenkinson, was passing in her phaeton at the time and her horse, being startled, added greater confusion and consternation to the scene. I apologised most profusely for the distress caused and promised to call on the ladies at Rosings at the first possible opportunity to make amends for my foolishness and to bring word of the arrival of our newborn. And having, the evening before, spilled coffee on Lady Lucas's satin gown, I was feeling it best to avoid all women by locking myself up in my study, until such time as I felt steadied (which, I confess, was never fully accomplished until after Thomas's arrival and, perhaps, not even then).

Thomas is a healthy boy, praise the Lord, and Sir William declares he has his chin, which Charlotte believes is possible, for he has many. I myself see a little of my late mother in him, especially around the eyes, for there is a cunning there which would appear to have skipped my generation but has resurfaced in Thomas, bless the boy. We are fortunate indeed and Charlotte is overjoyed and glad to have her mother with her at this time.

I feel all the weight of additional responsibilities now landing on my shoulders, for I have an example to set as a father to both my child and the parishioners and it is a duty I will take most seriously, for any misdemeanours and little human weaknesses which I had heretofore indulged in, must now be plucked out and cast away.

Mrs Collins joins me in extending an invitation to your family to visit us here at our humble abode at your earliest possible convenience. It has been my greatest wish, since our two families have become so intimate and in order to repay the frequent generosity shown to me at Longbourn, to invite you hither. As my cousin Elizabeth, nay, I must call her Mrs Darcy, is to join her husband in visiting Rosings at Easter, it is our dearest wish that you, Mrs Bennet and your daughters will coincide their visit with a stay with us. We may be a compact company but, if the girls are willing to share a room, and we use the closets (now that they have shelves therein) for storage and accept every request to dine at Rosings, you will find that this parsonage can comfortably accommodate us all.

Indeed, another motive for my inviting you hither is to restore harmony at Rosings, for your presence may soften her ladyship's disposition toward Elizabeth (it will be her first time accepting my cousin into Rosings as a guest since the undesireable union between her and Mr Darcy). When Lady Catherine becomes more acquainted with the respectable family from whence she comes, I am confident that all relations will be amiable and delightful. Her charitable and forgiving nature appears to have already put the sad business behind her although Charlotte states that it is because she has now turned her attentions to her other nephew, Colonel Fitzwilliam, as a future son-in-law. In truth, I cannot say.

Sir, again we are blessed in Thomas. The future of

Longbourn is secured for another generation and please give all your dear family our sincerest well-wishes and we hope to see you at Easter.

Your cousin,

William Collins

Longbourn,
near Meryton,
Hertfordshire.

19th February, 1793

Dear Sir,

On behalf of all at Longbourn, may I extend the heartiest congratulations to you and Charlotte on the birth of young Thomas Lewis Henry Collins. We are delighted and have toasted his good health.

It was not your letter from Kent which informed us, however, of your happy news but my sister-in-law, Mrs Philips, from Meryton. She called on Mrs Bennet last week in her usual ostentatious manner, that forever sends me to the garden or my library for refuge, and announced in a deafening tone (that reminded me of a cannon I once heard fired on Hove beach, to warn off smugglers) that the Collinses had welcomed a boy, Thomas, into the world. We never question her source of information for she mixes with high and low alike, but we can vouch that she is never wrong. The inclusion of 'Henry' in his naming has not gone undetected by me and I am deeply touched to the core of my being. I also noticed that Lady Catherine's late husband, Lewis, gets a nod and am sure he is equally flattered, wherever he may now be found.

But, sir, I must insist, please do not undertake further correspondence until your wrist, is healed. I implore you to throw etiquette to one side and use the well-thought-of common sense of a rational man. In fact, I hereby declare we are honoured and accept your kind invitation to stay and give you the date of our expected arrival at Easter, and that no further communication is necessary until then. Mrs Bennet, who is truly delighted with the invitation, Kitty, Mary and I arrive on Spy Wednesday, March 23rd, and stay for ten nights, if that is not too great an inconvenience to your household. We will keep to ourselves, as best we can, that we are not in your way. Mary and I will be satisfied with a book, while Kitty will be drawn to Rosings at every opportunity by Mrs Bennet, to spend time with Elizabeth (who is now with child) and to be awestruck by her surroundings and, therefore, cousin, you will hardly discern we are about.

As for your most generous offer to bring a collection of your sermons with you to Longbourn, I must stipulate, sir, that I will hear none of it. Those sermons, so sanctified and divinely inspired, were meant for the ears of your parishioners and especially for the benefit of Lady Catherine de Bourgh and her household. I would feel like I was trespassing, nay, stealing from her, to listen to them so, please, ease my conscience by relinquishing this most kind offer.

In the interim, I will keep an inquisitive eye out for the return of Sir William and Lady Lucas, that they should bring us tidings of young Thomas. Best wishes again to your dear wife, Charlotte, and all at Hunsford.

Yours sincerely,

Henry Bennet

Longbourn,
near Meryton,
Hertfordshire.

6th April, 1793

Dear Mr Collins,

I write now to inform you of our safe arrival home and to thank you for your unprecedented kindness to us on our recent stay with you at Hunsford Parsonage during Easter and your kind introduction of the Bennet family to all at Rosings.

Little has changed in our absence excepting we lost our dear old apple tree, the one I could see here from my library window. Apparently, the storm had not been severe but, as you pointed out to me on several occasions, it was diseased beyond measure and should really have been taken down long before now. It was something I refused to do, similar in a way to putting down a loyal old dog – when it came to the time, I just had not the heart. I always felt "she has another year in her yet!" The girls did swing from that tree throughout their childhood and I found it gave me comfort to look on it. Nature, however, in her wisdom did see fit to take matters into her own hands but, at least, had the benevolence to wait until I was absent. It is now in the fireplace and keeping me warm as I write to you now.

I believed Mary, being so fond of nature and forever in the garden, would weep but she did not. She explained that all the cycles of nature are good and part of God's plan, therefore not to be mourned. A singular lady, our Mary! I suspect her of planning an escape to a convent on the continent when I depart for I have seen particular books and observed letters despatched. I have not mentioned it to her for I feel it gives her comfort as she sips tea with neighbours to dream of cloisters and solitude.

Thomas is indeed a fine fellow. I look forward with eagerness to his growth and development to discover whether he inherits the Collins intelligence and eloquence or the Lucas practicality and chins. Either way, it will be an interesting collaboration of traits and demeanours.

We stopped for a night with the Gardiners in London, as planned, for the roads are bad after the winter and we were tired. I must confess, though they meant well by getting tickets for us for Covent Garden, I had much rather stay at home. I felt *The London Gazette* and a new port that Mr Gardiner had recently acquired were calling to me but, alas, I was forced to ignore, nay neglect, them and move where I was not wanted nor where there was any appeal for me.

Fortunately, however, I did witness an incident that turned the evening around in my estimation and provided real entertainment. I noticed a young gentleman sitting in a row where the seating was steep, who appeared to have as much interest in the dramatics on stage as I had, for his head kept nodding as though he were falling asleep. It dawned on me that perhaps he was on to something and that, when confident of being unobserved, I could follow his example in time. I kept a watch and at last he fell into a slumber only to awake, moments later, upside-down in the lap of the lady in front. I could not tell who was more alarmed for many, including the gentleman himself, were screaming. All we could see were his legs in the air and two persons attempting to retrieve him back to his seat and all was uproar for some minutes. Although many consoled the lady, my sympathies lay with the poor, embarrassed man and a silent prayer of gratitude escaped my lips, as I looked at the lady in the row in front of myself, "there but for the Grace of God goes Mr Bennet".

Speaking of young gentlemen, that Colonel Fitzwilliam is a very likeable chap. He seemed to be quite taken with our Kitty whenever we dined at Rosings although I believe Lady Catherine now has her sights set on him to marry her daughter, fortune not being an issue in that household. A very nice chap indeed, I believe he stays with Darcy at Pemberley a great deal. He and Darcy, who has grown considerably on me, are very fond of each other, more like brothers than cousins, and Elizabeth, never having a brother of her own, also seems attached to the young soldier. Mrs Bennet is insisting that Kitty joins Elizabeth at Pemberley from Michaelmas to Christmas, to ensure that she has a companion after the arrival of her child, to be joined by the rest of us at Christmas.

Enough of these matters for now. Wishing you and your dear family all the best.

Your affectionate cousin,

Henry Bennet

Hunsford,
near Westerham,
Kent.

5th May, 1793

Dear Sir,

I am most glad that you arrived home safely and sorry to hear that you lost your most favoured apple tree. Indeed, it was a miracle that it has survived thus far. In fact, I was quite afraid to walk anywhere in the proximity of it on my last trip into Hertfordshire, lest it fall over or a bough break and fall upon my head.

I do hope you are utterly mistaken in your opinion of Mary … such suspicions should be investigated at once, and no leniency shown, for it is a grave sin no lesser than that committed by her sister, Lydia. I have, however, always found Mary to be very knowledgeable in the doctrines and writings of the Church of England and to have a strong sense of her obligation to her family, therefore I am confident that you are incorrect in assuming that she would turn her back on her faith for the mere lure of quietude.

I am obliged, cousin, to turn now, however, to a subject of the most serious nature. As you may recall, I was horrified to find myself on the receipt of Lady Catherine's rage and disapproval following the engagement of Mr Darcy and my fair cousin Elizabeth last year. It was several months before she would permit me into her company or acknowledge me following Sunday service and many more weeks before she would invite us to dine at Rosings. Indeed she is only now allowing those dishes, which she knows to be my favourites, to appear at table when we dine.

It is, therefore, with the utmost solemnity that I must insist that you interfere at once in any plans my cousin Catherine may have regarding visiting at Pemberley and meeting Colonel Fitzwilliam again. The reasons I have are as follows: firstly that it is widely known that Colonel Fitzwilliam must marry for wealth. As a second son, he has not the fortune of his elder brother or of his cousins Mr Darcy and his sister Georgiana Darcy or his cousin Miss Anne de Bourgh. Although he has a wealthy uncle in Madeira who is known to be very unwell and not expected to live very long, it is also known, through Lady Catherine's contacts, that his immense fortune is to be divided in five betwixt all his nieces and nephews, thereby improving Colonel Fitzwilliam's situation but not sufficiently to suit his manner of living.

The second reason is that he is intended for Miss Anne de Bourgh and although it is a peculiar engagement of sorts, whereby he is not aware of the particulars, the subject is to be broached and finalised on his next visit to Rosings with Lady Catherine, herself, expected to make the announcement at Christmas.

The final reason, sir, is for my sake. On receiving your last letter, I felt it best to make haste at once to Rosings to inform Lady Catherine that there was something sinister afoot but she at once flew into a rage, similar to that which I witnessed in the past, making me regret that I had said anything at all. I was, yet again, to blame! I had brought the Bennets to Rosings and introduced them to her eligible nephew, I who knew their cunning ways and crafty manner of procuring husbands. I was, she said to my horror, determined to bring down the house of Rosings and see the future of the finest families in the country destroyed.

I will say no more on this subject, sir, excepting that I expect, as the future heir of Longbourn, to have my wishes met on this very important issue.

With kind regards to Mrs Bennet and all at Longbourn.

Yours sincerely,

William Collins

Hunsford,
near Westerham,
Kent.

31st July, 1793

Dear Mr Bennet,

I do hope that all my cousins at Longbourn are well this summer and that you received my last correspondence of early May. I fear it may have been lost, for I have been waiting patiently for a response which has not arrived and, as it held such important advice, I shall attempt to abbreviate here that you can proceed to take action immediately.

I beg that you will write to me, at your very earliest convenience, with a reassurance that my cousin Catherine will not be staying at Pemberley between Michaelmas and Christmas, for to risk tempting a certain young gentleman, who stays there often, but whose affections are engaged elsewhere.

I am confident that you understand of what I speak and if you did receive my last correspondence all the very valid and legitimate reasons for preventing any future meetings between the pair are laid out clearly.

I am optimistic in expecting your response without delay.
Yours sincerely,

William Collins

Longbourn,
near Meryton,
Hertfordshire.

17th October, 1793

Dear Sir,

Sincere apologies for the delay in writing to you but I found myself very busy this summer. Our harvest was good, praise the Lord, though the work was difficult. As the weather was fine, we arranged a dance and feast of sorts on the last day for all the workers. They were a merry crew as the cider was plentiful and flowing and, I must confess, I felt obliged (and in the company of your father-in-law, Sir William) to join in the festivities and fun. We had quite a time of it, I can tell you! I had not seen Sir William as jovial since his wedding day, many years ago (in fact I did see him dance with a teapot as the night came to a close).

And I assume that you may have heard the wonderful news that we have become grandparents two months since. Elizabeth and Darcy had a baby girl, Rebecca, and all are well. Mrs Bennet and I are delighted and so much more looking forward to our visit to Pemberley at Christmas. Kitty keeps us up to date with all that has occurred and dotes on her niece. I believe your fears, of which you wrote in such great detail, regarding Kitty and a certain gentleman are totally unfounded. I am sure I will be confirming as much in my next correspondence at Christmas, so do not write until then as it is only a few short weeks away.

We now must sit tight and wait patiently for Jane and

Bingley to deliver us our next grandchild in the New Year and then we'll be off to another fine country house to make a further nuisance of ourselves. We have not yet been to Clarinda Park but Mrs Bennet assures me it is reputed to have one of the finest collections of silver in England and that, apparently, is a very great thing.

With all our dear wishes to Charlotte, Thomas and all your friends and neighbours.

Your cousin,

Henry Bennet

Pemberley Estate,
Derbyshire.

20th December, 1793

Dear Sir,

May I wish you and all at Hunsford parsonage the most happy and peaceful of Christmases and a prosperous New Year.

I hardly know how to write this, as I know you to have been vehemently against the match, but broach the subject I must. Our dear Kitty and Colonel Fitzwilliam are engaged. We are, of course, as her doting parents, delighted for them both and hope that, in time, you will feel similarly.

In response to your previous letter and three concerns you had regarding the match, I respond as follows in the hope it will alleviate your fears. Firstly, that it would appear that Colonel Fitzwilliam's uncle in Madeira, as you so wisely predicted, has moved onto his heavenly reward and bequeathed Colonel Fitzwilliam with not one-fifth but three-fifths of his fortune, omitting both Darcy and Georgiana from the will. Seemingly, some years ago, both Darcy and his sister, deciding that their wealth was substantial enough, felt it proper to increase the fortune of their dear friend and cousin by requesting, from their uncle, that their share be passed onto him. So now, Colonel Fitzwilliam is an independent gentleman who may marry where he pleases.

Your second objection was that he was in some way engaged to his cousin, Miss Anne de Bourgh, with an announcement due at Christmas. It would appear that on his most recent visit to Rosings the subject was indeed broached but as the engagement was of an imaginary and fictitious nature, with the groom-to-be unaware of its existence, its end was swift.

As for the final objection, I confess, sir, I am truly sorry to be the bearer of news that will guarantee you the displeasure of distressing your patroness once again. All I can say is that Lady Catherine is in error when accusing you of the enormity of causing two young people to fall in love. Surely, free will, for which Adam and Eve ate of that apple, had a small part to play in it.

Indeed, I was saddened that you felt it necessary to remind me of your position as heir to Longbourn, as if that very fact would amend my actions, that I would fear for the future of my wife and children and act against my conscience, but, as you can see, they are all, but one, well married now and so shall not be destitute on my departure from this world.

I hope, dear cousin, that we can put this issue behind us and be happy for the betrothed couple. I expect you will be taking cover in Lucas Lodge soon, once the news breaks at Rosings. We return to Longbourn ourselves within the week, so please come join us for dinner when you have come and are settled.

Again a very happy Christmas to one and all.

Your cousin,

Henry Bennet

Hunsford,
near Westerham,
Kent.

29th December, 1793

Dear Sir,

Having just come now from Rosings, it is with regret but steadfastness that I feel called upon as a servant of the Church of England to denounce your calculating manner of securing a husband for your daughter, in which several of the Ten Commandments are, to all effects and purposes, disregarded. Sir, I have no doubt that you were aware of what you were about when sending Catherine to Pemberley and that you would do so, against my express wishes and knowing the pain and distress it would cause at both Hunsford and Rosings, has rocked the very foundations of my faith in humanity.

I can confirm that Lady Catherine de Bourgh is outraged and is gone now to Pemberley to break the engagement. That my noble patroness, worthy of my gratitude and reverence, a thousand times over, is risking her life, to travel to Pemberley during such horrendous weather and in the heart of winter, would be a burden on the conscience of any good Christian.

Time will reveal what the outcome of this sad affair will be but I must say, sir, that I am deeply and seriously displeased that my hand is forced to write such a letter as this. You are in error in assuming that we shall be taking cover at Lucas Lodge as it is our intention to remain loyally and resolutely at Hunsford to offer our support to Rosings during this distressing time.

Your cousin,

William Collins

1794 — the year in which an unfortunate breach of friendship transpires between Mr Collins and Mr Bennet.

Longbourn,
near Meryton,
Hertfordshire.

3rd January, 1794

Dear Sir,

I find I must write to you of my amusement on reading your last correspondence. That I am accused of forcing Lady Catherine de Bourgh of Rosings Park, Kent (a woman renowned for knowing her own mind) into her carriage on the coldest day of winter and slapping the hinds of her horses that they may gallop at high-speed in the direction of Pemberley is quite simply comical.

I also find it remarkable that you believe it the duty of a random country gentleman, such as myself, to be seen running down every country lane in England, jumping between any young man and woman who should take a liking to each other. I assure you, sir, I have more important affairs to attend to. I had much rather, for example, tend to my blackcurrant bush.

And as for breaking the Ten Commandments, I believe it may be a case of the pot calling the kettle black, for it is you, cousin, so preoccupied with bowing, genuflecting and curtseying in the direction of Rosings, to the absolute neglect of all your clerical obligations to your other parishioners, who must be accused of committing idolatry.

Wishing you, your family and all at Rosings the happiest of New Years.

Sincerely,

Henry Bennet

Hunsford,
near Westerham,
Kent.

7th January, 1794

Dear Sir,

I have had much time to reflect on this dreadful affair, having lost many nights' sleep in recent months, and, as you must now be aware, Lady Catherine de Bourgh was unsuccessful in her breaking of the engagement. It will be of no interest to you to learn that I am shaken to the core and even my dear Charlotte, she of a calm disposition in the norm, finds herself truly distressed at this time.

And no matter how earnestly I attempt to read your most recent correspondence in a different light, there is no escaping the fact that you have insulted me in every manner conceivable which regrettably confirms my father's judgement of the Bennet family as being correct. I was in error attempting, though my intentions were honourable and just, to bridge that divide and dishonour his memory and wishes.

I believe it is best to say no more on this matter at present or in the future.

William Collins

Longbourn,
near Meryton,
Hertfordshire.

31st March, 1794

Dear Sir,

I hope this letter finds you all well at Hunsford. You most likely heard through Elizabeth and Charlotte's correspondence that Jane and Bingley welcomed a baby girl, Martha, into the world. All are well, thank goodness. We go to visit them shortly for the Easter season.

How does your vegetable patch come along?

Yours sincerely,

Henry Bennet

Longbourn,
near Meryton,
Hertfordshire.

28th September, 1794

Dear Sir,

My best wishes to you, Charlotte and all your family this Michaelmas.

You may be happy to hear that we had another good harvest this year, praise the Lord. The Longbourn Estate becomes more productive with each passing year.

Your father-in-law, Sir William, has agreed to assist us in celebrating with the workers as has become his custom and has even been so kind as to suggest that I request one of your fine passages to be recited as thanksgiving for our abundant blessings.

I hope that you will agree to this request, especially as Sir William was so pleased with his suggestion and adamant that a blessing given by his son-in-law and future heir of Longbourn would be most appropriate, in which I wholeheartedly concur.

Yours sincerely,

Henry Bennet

Longbourn,
near Meryton,
Hertfordshire.

31st November, 1794

Dear Mr Collins,

May I take this opportunity to wish you and all at Hunsford the very best of the season as Christmas approaches and takes over our lives.

We had a delightful time at Clarinda Park with Jane, Bingley and the lovely Martha. She has inherited her parents' temperament, her aunt Miss Bingley's fondness for items that sparkle and her grandmother's habit of babbling to herself. Elizabeth and family came to stay for a number of nights during our visit which was a lovely thing for us all. A small dance was held in our honour which added an air of excitement and gentility – a far cry from a dance at our brother and sister Philips, who bring all ranks together. I have heard it said that a young lady may attend a party at the Philipses' and leave engaged, to either a prince or a thief, or both.

Though it is a matter which pains me, I feel obliged to broach the subject of our falling out over this past twelve-month. On mature recollection, Mr Collins, I do believe myself to have been too harsh in my comments and wish now to approach your charitable nature and request a reconciliation. In truth, I miss our correspondence and though I hear much of your news from Elizabeth or the Lucases, such as your waiting on the birth of a second child, I had much rather hear it from yourself that I may congratulate you and Charlotte personally.

It also pained me to learn that you did have a short stay at Lucas Lodge recently and did not call on us during that time. I would have liked to meet young Thomas again for I hear from Sir William that he has an adventurous spirit.

I hope this letter finds you, and all yours, in good health.

Your affectionate cousin,

Henry Bennet

1795 — the year in which an olive branch is accepted, a visitor comes to Rosings, a scandalous situation arises and a most auspicious wedding takes place.

Hunsford,
near Westerham,
Kent.

31ˢᵗ January, 1795

Dear Sir,

Please accept this correspondence as an acknowledgement of receipt of your letter last November and confirmation that an attempt to heal the breach standing between our two families would be satisfactory to me. Much as I find so many grounds for acting to the contrary, I believe it is my duty, as a servant of God and in accordance with my nature, which tends towards charity, forgiveness and benevolence, to make every effort to accept the olive branch which you now extend. I will proceed with resolve and attempt to re-establish those ties, though they may be permanently and irretrievably damaged, that once were a great comfort to us both.

Fortunately, I have some wonderful news to impart which is adding to my current generous humour, though it concerns the residents of Rosings Park and, therefore, shall be of little interest to you. Miss Anne de Bourgh is engaged to be married. As you may remember, twelve months since, it had been Lady Catherine's dearest wish to announce her daughter's engagement to her nephew, Colonel Fitzwilliam, which alas was not to be, for reasons which shall not be uttered at this delicate juncture. I can confirm, however, that a much superior match has been made with a gentleman of greater standing in society and all are overjoyed.

And so I found myself busy again this Christmas and New

Year season with all the additional duties of my parish, tending to my dear Charlotte during this time of expectancy, together with perfecting my passages for one of the most prominent weddings of the decade. I go to Oxford soon, having been invited by the esteemed Reverend Edmund Smellie. I shall tell you more in my next correspondence.

Please pass on the regards of myself and my dear family to all at Longbourn this New Year.

Your cousin,

William Collins

Longbourn,
near Meryton,
Hertfordshire.

14th February, 1795

Dear Sir,

Let me commence by wishing you, Charlotte, Thomas and now young Richard Lewis Collins the very best of health. I have learned from the Lucases, who are hitching up their horses even now as I write, that he is a hale and hearty boy and that Charlotte is very well indeed. It is always a relief to know that all are out of danger for, although we know them to be the stronger and more intelligent of the sexes, the ladies must receive extra care at this time and I have no doubt that you and your household are being extra vigilant and mindful of Charlotte's needs. I have noticed how the late Lewis de Bourgh's name features yet again in your latest offspring's name and believe that the honour will not go unacknowledged by his widow.

I must say that your last letter was indeed a great comfort to me and has eased my mind considerably. I have not been my usual unflustered self for some time, due to our disagreement, whereby even Mrs Bennet became concerned as the months continued. She observed that I was more withdrawn than usual, with an extra tightness about my forehead, and declared that it was a sign that I was on the verge of an apoplectic fit, offering me use of the back room and her smelling salts, if ever I felt an episode coming on. Even with her daughters well married, dear Mrs Bennet is fond of having me about and is not ready to part with me yet. I am grateful that you have accepted the olive branch and let us say no more of the matter as we turn over a new leaf.

We were quite unaware of the wonderful news regarding Miss de Bourgh's engagement and found that Sir William's knowledge of the particulars are sadly lacking, with the exception that the fortunate gentleman hails from a great house in the midlands where knights are a-plenty. Perhaps you will be so kind as to inform us of the details as we would like to toast to their health and happiness and, of course, let me know how your great passages are progressing.

As you have no doubt heard through Elizabeth's correspondence with your wife, we now have many grandchildren. Jane, as you know, has Martha and is with child again. Lizzy has Rebecca and now Charles. Lydia has had a boy called George, named after his father (so that we may be ever reminded of the scoundrel) and our Kitty is expectant at present. Mrs Bennet assures me they are all the most wonderful children in the land and furnishes me with such particulars as to their size, weight and colouring but, as I remind her, unless she is speaking to me of geese, calves or foals, she wastes her breath.

It is unusually mild for this time of year which bodes well for your voyage to Oxford, of which I am most curious. I wonder how this weather will affect my fruit trees.

With fondest regards,

Henry Bennet

Hunsford,
near Westerham,
Kent.

13th March, 1795

My Dear Sir,

Please accept my best wishes for all at Longbourn. We are all well and delighting in our latest blessing, young Richard. Praise the Lord yet again.
I enclose a book now which I purchased on my recent visit to Oxford which will be a great addition to the library at Longbourn. It is the inspiring work by my host in Oxford, the Reverend Edmund Smellie, An Unabridged Guide to the One Thousand, Seven Hundred and Sixty-Three Sins listed in the Old and New Testaments. *He encouraged me to buy several copies, that I may enlighten and educate those within my sphere of influence. It is cleverly written in alphabetical order, which is a great aid to the reader, but let me warn you, cousin, there are some sins which would not be appropriate for the eyes of your young ladies, so perhaps the top shelf of your library is its most fitting home for now. Mary, in particular, would possibly be drawn to this worthy ecumenical work but again, perhaps, you had better shield her from familiarising herself with its contents. I, myself, am still attempting to come to an understanding regarding a number of the 'sins' and have written, this very morning, to the esteemed author that he may enlighten me, so if you find yourself encountering similar difficulties, please let me know that I can inform and instruct you likewise.*

My recent trip to Oxford was at the request of the aforementioned Reverend Edmund Smellie, writer and orator, of whom you have no doubt heard by now. His sermon 48 "Who will rise up with me against the wicked?" Psalm 94:16, published in The London Gazette *last year, created quite a fuss and, I believe, is borrowed by every esteemed clergyman of repute in the country. Indeed, I make no secret of the fact that I have, on occasion, slipped in a number of phrases from the aforementioned sermon to strengthen my words for I find that the Holy Spirit inspired me to do so – that the Word of God might pierce more hearts and more deeply.*

I was quite startled to receive his invitation for though we had studied together at Oxford, even sharing a room at one point during our carefree youth, I had not known that he held me in such high regard. I must confess that I did not approve of all his undertakings back then and did find myself obliged to close my eyes to much of his activities and the company he kept. He has since, however, risen so swiftly within the Church of England and is now regarded as one of the most pious, moving and influential speakers in the whole country, that he has earned my esteem and respect. Indeed, Lady Catherine de Bourgh, who had once witnessed Rev Smellie, in the height of his fame, speak at the consecration of her cousin the Archbishop of Canterbury, was so impressed to hear that he was an acquaintance of mine that she pressed me to go to Oxford at once and extend an invitation for him to stay. Not at Hunsford, as one might expect, but at Rosings and at his earliest possible convenience. I believe Sir Lewis de Bourgh was a great follower of the works of Reverend Smellie and had kept all his published works in his fine library, which has an extensive collection, particularly on its top shelves.

I also had the privilege of observing Rev. Smellie perform one of his great sermons during my recent trip and was so moved and shaken as a result, that it was many hours before I could settle myself and re-admit myself to his presence. Not that I would have been able, should I have wished, for there was such a flock about him, ladies in particular, who had wild eyes and were half-swooning at his every utterance.

He kindly offered advice as to how I should deliver my great passages in a similar fashion, for I made him aware that the wedding of Miss Anne de Bourgh approaches, which I expect will be my finest hour. His key recommendation was to practise in front of a looking glass, that one may rehearse one's demeanour and perfect one's facial movements, for, he assured me, with every twitch of one's mouth, arch of an eyebrow and pointing a finger to Heaven, one shall strike fear in the hearts of men and serenity to their souls.

And as for the impending marriage of Miss Anne de Bourgh, let me enlighten you as to the name and character of the most fortunate gentleman in the land. It is Harold, son of Lord and Lady Smock of Eyrecourt Castle in Warwickshire, a most accomplished young man (considering he is of ill-health) who keeps the largest collection of butterflies and moths in the land. Indeed, he is such an expert on the subject that his knowledge and advice are sought after by the greatest minds in Europe and, I believe, he is in correspondence with a university in America who, Lady Catherine informs me, are very interested in his 'Banded Peacock'. Miss de Bourgh is almost animated whenever the wedding is mentioned (young ladies do love a sense of occasion) and once Mr Smock (accompanied by his parents) is well enough for the long journey to Rosings, the date will be set. Then my great passages will be taken out of my bureau drawer for to be extensively re-read, reviewed, revised and rehearsed, for

Lady Catherine has requested that I officiate at the wedding ceremony.

The happy couple have not yet met in person but have corresponded by letter and I believe they are very much attached to one another. I have, myself, made a few very eloquent suggestions to Miss de Bourgh, via her companion, Mrs Jenkinson, for inclusion in her correspondence, for who more than I knows those words and phrases which quicken the heart and flatter the soul.

On another topic, I must ask you now, cousin, whether persons in your vicinity are wont to play practical jokes on your rector, Reverend Green? I find myself, yet again, troubled by such blackguarding and it vexes me so. Yesterday, as I left the premises for my morning stroll in the magnificent Rosings air, I found, to my horror, that two of my garden ornaments (you may remember the swans with wings outstretched which you had once admired for the breadth of their wingspan) were rendered to the top of my two piers at the entrance to Hunsford Parsonage. They are stuck solid and will have to be broken asunder in order to have them removed which John, our gardener, is doing as I write, though the sweat is pouring from his brow. When it occurred yesterday morn, I moved at once to Rosings Park to tell her ladyship, who was naturally outraged. I informed her that I suspect the culprit is a Mr Joseph Bradford, one of those idle gentlemen residing in the cottages in the village, for he walked past as I made my discovery and laughed so heartily, saying that my piers were now as fine as her ladyship's, that I felt it were he for sure.

That is all our news from Kent for now. Again, young Richard is a blessing and a quiet boy thus far, praise the Lord, and Thomas grows more characterful daily.

Our kindest regards to dear Mrs Bennet and all your esteemed family.

Your affectionate cousin,

William Collins

Longbourn,
near Meryton,
Hertfordshire.

4th April, 1795

Dear Sir,

I hope this letter finds you and yours in the best of health this Easter Sunday morning. Thank you for your kind gesture – the Reverend Smellie's fine book. I have leafed through it while sipping a glass of port the other evening and I must confess it was a mistake for I almost choked as the port went down the wrong passageway. He must have been a colourful character indeed, this friend of yours, Rev. Smellie, for he wrote in such minute detail, never tempering his vocabulary, that I felt he must needs know his subject matter very well indeed. And fear not that I might need any explanation for I have such a son-in-law in George Wickham who can enlighten me on any or every one of its contents, I have no doubt.

What an unusual turn of events that this Reverend Smellie did track you down after all these years. No doubt he was impressed on hearing the name of your noble patroness and is a very fortunate man indeed to receive an invitation to Rosings.

I have met with Reverend Green this very morning as he came by with a vintage French wine (the French may trouble Lord Nelson but they do have some redeeming qualities and, I dare say, if he would drink of their fine wines it would lessen his grievance with their nation). I inquired of the good vicar whether he were the recipient of an occasional practical joke and he assures me that he is not. Fear not, however, Mr Collins, for this man is quite doting and would not know whether a joke were being played on him or not. In fact, I believe I was, back in my youth, the culprit responsible for rounding up and placing nine wild cats in his bedroom where he discovered them in a state of war and destruction some hours later.

But on to more interesting matters – would you believe that the reputation of young Harold Smock, the son of Lord and Lady Smock of Eyrecourt Castle, is already known to me? For was I not only last week reading from the great book *Insects of South America* wherein it mentioned that this very Harold, of whom you speak, is the owner of the only example of Morpho Menelaus Alexandrovna in the Northern Hemisphere at present! Can you imagine my surprise on reading your letter? I would be most interested in making his acquaintance, cousin, if you would be so kind as to introduce us at some future juncture, for I have many questions to put to him as to the survival of butterflies in countries of high altitude such as Peru. It has troubled me for some time and I have not yet found an answer that satisfied my curiosity. I am all delight for Miss Anne de Bourgh that she has secured such a husband for I can only imagine what interesting things they may have to say to each other.

For now, cousin, adieu!

Henry Bennet

Hunsford,
near Westerham,
Kent.

14th May, 1795

Dear Sir,

I hope this letter finds you and all your household well this fine summer day. I must confess I hardly know whether I come or go in recent times for with the impending arrival next week of the Reverend Edmund Smellie to Rosings, waiting on news regarding the health and mobility of the honourable Smock family, and an unfortunate incident which brought me into a most disagreeable situation, I hardly know where I am.

The incident I refer to took place last Tuesday teatime as I returned from an afternoon in the garden – Charlotte has been encouraging me to spend as much time in the fresh air as daylight allows, assuring me that it is now the fashionable practice of educated gentlemen. As I went to pick up my garden shears from the front lawn where I had left them not twenty minutes before, I found they had gone. Just at that moment, the blackguard, Joseph Bradford, was passing and made such a wave in my direction, bellowing "Are you looking for something, Mr Collins?" that I was convinced at once that he had stolen my shears. I ran immediately to Rosings, distressed and agitated, to inform her ladyship of this wrongdoing. As magistrate she was doubly furious, for this was no joke but a crime, and, therefore, she prepared at once to go to Bradford's cottage that she might interrogate the culprit to his face (for it is few who do not break down and confess when confronted by her ladyship). I was ordered home to drink a glass of cognac to counter the effects of shock. Her ladyship promised to summons me to Rosings for dinner in the evening where she would inform me of the outcome of her investigation. I was very moved that she would condescend to act with such purpose and bring such trouble on herself on behalf of a lowly vicar and I must confess, sir, never was my loyalty and affection for her as great as it was at that moment, that it did bring tears to my eyes.

When I returned home, I consumed two glasses of cognac as ordered and, I must confess, their mellowing effect was felt almost immediately. I then proceeded to check on the boys and Charlotte who were all to be found at the front of the house playing skittles. Charlotte, alarmed at my appearance and smelling the liquor on my breath, demanded to know at once what I was about to make a display of myself in front of our boys, whereupon hearing of my troubles she declared that it was she who had removed the shears from the front lawn for fear the boys would find them and injure themselves. My shock was great and it was some moments before I could comprehend the seriousness of what I was hearing. I ran at once to Bradford's cottage where I found I was too late – her ladyship, with raised voice, which I could hear before I had even reached the front gate, was accusing the man of being a liar and a thief who would be dragged before the courts and feel the full force of her wrath. I waited until she was returning to her carriage where I whispered to her, with trepidation, of the error I had made. Cousin, she called me such names, degraded me in such terms and uninvited me to dinner as left no doubt in my mind as to her displeasure. When she departed, I felt obliged to return to Bradford and scold him for angering her ladyship in such a manner. I stated that while the charges against him would be dropped, he had better not be seen in the vicinity of my parsonage again or it would surely be Van Dieman's Land for him if he proceeded to act in dishonest ways, at which he merely laughed in my face.

The silence from Rosings continues and I hope it will be mended by the time Reverend Smellie arrives next week for I so wished to impress Lady Catherine with my standing within the higher echelons of the Church of England.

Yours sincerely,

William Collins

Longbourn,
near Meryton,
Hertfordshire.

30th May, 1795

My Dear Sir,

Having just this evening re-read your most recent letter, I decided to drink several glasses of cognac in an attempt at commiserating with you in your current plight, displaying solidarity for my own flesh and blood and finally because your letter put me in mind of the French and a bottle of cognac which I had almost forgot that I had. I confess up front, I find myself very much merry at present, but shall proceed with this letter regardless, for I am feeling particularly philosophical this starry night and full of steely determination and not to be swayed.

What a most unfortunate thing to bring the wrath of her ladyship upon yourself yet again. Of course, I have not seen her in such a humour, she is all sweetness and charm whenever we meet, but my imaginative capabilities are very great and I have no doubt that she is fierce when riled. Indeed Admiral Nelson could do with just a few of her ladyships on board when dealing with the French and victory would be certain, but not before a few trunks of their best cognac is secured to the mast, I say! Did you know that many shipments of cognac are distributed around Europe from the port of La Rochelle in France where the Romans set up house and home many years ago and began salt production along the coast? There are few advances in man's development and industries,

I find, that the Romans had not thought of first. There are many who do not want to hear of this, especially the men of science and invention and the money-grabbing mill owners and city merchants, but I dare say we will discover, in time, that the Romans had invented everything many thousands of years before they dawned on us. Which puts me in mind that I was often told that I am the proprietor of a Roman nose – they tend to be large, with a distinct bump at the top causing them to curve somewhat, similar to the bird who lives along the coast called a puffin. There is a young French soldier, of whom we read about in the newspapers as rising swiftly up the ranks in his military career, by the name of Napoleon Bonaparte whom they claim has such a nose. But the Greek nose, now that is a very non-descript feature which adds no distinction whatsoever to the face; it may as well not be there at all. But your own nose, Mr Collins, being bulbous, adds plenty of character to your face and suits you perfectly for if a person takes one look at your face, cousin, they have your character in an instant.

Enough of noses. I hope that all the Smocks of the castle in Warwickshire will be making their way to Rosings soon and that young Harold's health remains strong for he is a man I wish to meet before long. Shall the married couple remain at Rosings or return to Warwickshire? And as for the Reverend Smellie, another man I would be curious to meet, he must be with you at least a week by now. I hope he is settling into life at Rosings and does not miss the fast life in Oxford.

Your affectionate cousin,

Henry Bennet

Hunsford,
near Westerham,
Kent.

14th June, 1795

Dear Sir,

I must confess this letter finds me very disturbed indeed and although I wish to make my usual and customary compliments to your good wife and family, I find I hardly have the strength of spirit to do so, for I am a broken man.

Lady Catherine's displeasure with me continues and although I was invited to Rosings to make the initial introduction of the Reverend Smellie to the family therein, I have hardly been invited back twice since then. Reverend Smellie appears to be enjoying his stay and the privileges bestowed upon him greatly and is a true favourite now (for he comes to visit me here at the parsonage every other day to inform me of his great fortune in minute detail). My dear Charlotte is also distressed for she has to increase her household expenditure as we dine and sup only here now and never feast elsewhere.

May I confess to you, Mr Bennet, something that I dare not say elsewhere. When he visited yesterday morning, Reverend Smellie asked of Charlotte that he might accompany her (alone) to the garden when she stated that she wished to collect lavender. My heart sank that he, who ladies find enthralling, would take such a liberty in front of me and my humiliation was great. Charlotte, however, loyal companion and wife amongst wives, knew at once the hurt he had intended. She returned from the kitchen with scissors and basket and handing them *to Reverend Smellie, pointed to him from the window the best patch, thanking him for sparing her the trouble. When he had left, red-faced at her treatment of him, Charlotte turned to me and stated that she never trusts a man whose hair appears to have the personality of an unruly child. My love for her was never greater than at that moment.*

But we have received news that Lord and Lady Smock and their son Harold leave Warwickshire on the morrow and are expected to arrive Thursday evening which is very great news indeed for the date of the wedding has been set for July 18th. This will enable me to redeem myself in the eyes of my noble patroness and re-establish my standing at Rosings.

My vegetable patch is sadly neglected.

Your cousin,

William Collins

Longbourn,
near Meryton,
Hertfordshire.

7th July, 1795

Dear Sir,

I am most sorry to read in your last correspondence of how disrupted and rattled you were as a result of Lady Catherine's cold shoulder – your heart, it seemed, was in your boots. Some might say that only a simpleton would invite such a man as Smellie into their territory where they should pillage and pluck as they wished, but not I. The whole affair is most disturbing, yet I am confident that it has even now blown over and you have been welcomed back to the warmth of her ladyship's affectionate embrace.

No doubt, as Miss de Bourgh's wedding day approaches, you are now rehearsing in front of the looking glass – those great passages which I always knew would see the light of day and fall on appreciative ears.

You might kindly whisper in the ear of Mr Smock, if he is not too preoccupied with wedding preparations, that he has a great admirer in Hertfordshire who has himself identified, in woodlands hereabouts, the High Brown Fritillary and can take him there some day if he ever finds himself in these parts that we may see if they breed thereabouts.

You will have heard that both Kitty and Jane have brought forth two healthy girls – Anne and Eliza respectively. All are well and we will be hitching up the horses again before the week is out, that we may make ourselves known to these little

creatures who neither know nor care for us yet.
My kindest regards to Charlotte and the boys.

Henry Bennet

Hunsford,
near Westerham,
Kent.

11th July, 1795

Dear Sir,

A quick message so very unlike my usual correspondence so please do not interpret it as rudeness on my part but, I am afraid to say, all is not well.

I am no longer to officiate at Miss Anne de Bourgh's wedding as that privilege now lies with Reverend Smellie. He was asked by Lady Catherine and accepted, without any consultation with myself, and all seem to have forgot that it was I who was to perform this privileged duty. I have been informed this morning by the very man himself who is all delight and wished to know, as there is little time to prepare, if he might borrow my great passages for the occasion, for he is very sure that he will not have to add a great deal to them to raise them to his usual standard. He said that I may join him at the altar for the final blessing, if I so wished, but he would not encourage it, for the comparison between myself and himself in front of my usual congregation might be too great and injure their opinion of me.

And to hear this when only yesterday Charlotte, she who is frequently wiser and more discerning than her husband, brought something to my attention that worried us both greatly. At her last visit at Rosings, Lady Catherine asked of her when we felt I would inherit the Longbourn Estate and move back into Hertfordshire. Charlotte replied that you, cousin, *are in great health and, although we enquire of your health frequently at Lucas Lodge, the response is always favourable. Later in their conversation, Lady Catherine complimented Charlotte on the improvements she has made at Hunsford, including the installation of a water pump at the side of the house, and said that she supposed it would be as comfortable for a single man who was accustomed to the conveniences of a large town as for a family of moderate means. And although I greatly respect the reputation and God-given gifts of Reverend Smellie, when I look at my two boys so happy at the parsonage, I feel it most keenly that we may be ousted soon and in this manner of degradation and betrayal.*

"I have sinned," he said, "for I have betrayed innocent blood." Matthew 27:3-4

Please extend my congratulations to Mr and Mrs Bingley and Colonel and Mrs Fitzwilliam on being blessed with two of God's children. I pray that they will never be crossed as I have been.

Your cousin,

William Collins

Longbourn,
near Meryton,
Hertfordshire.

7th September, 1795

Dear Sir,

We have just returned from our travels on Monday and are weary. We stayed first with the good-natured Bingleys, where we were joined by the bickering Wickhams (although George Junior is like neither his mother nor father) and next with the Fitzwilliams, who are delighting in parenthood, from whence we all travelled the short distance to Pemberley. And as fine and large as Pemberley is, Longbourn has never looked more charming nor my library more inviting as it did on our return, for I am tired of smiling at strangers and family alike. As the astute Thomas à Kempis once said, no doubt after a long pilgrimage himself, *"Everywhere I have sought peace and not found it, except in a corner with a book."* I feel that he and I would have been the best of friends – his company would be no trouble to me whatsoever.

But, sir, I am confused, for I have only now on my return received your last correspondence dated July 11th which concerned me greatly. In the first instance, I was alarmed that Lady Catherine looks forward to my demise with such enthusiasm and secondly, that you, if I may put it to you directly, are being overthrown by Smellie. I confess that I feared as much from the start – that his intentions were self-serving and that he was possibly reacquainting himself with you in order to take advantage of your connection with Rosings. And the sheer audacity of the man to request your great passages! But just as this information was sinking into my cerebrum, Sir William Lucas appeared on my doorstep to announce that Miss Anne de Bourgh did get wed but it was you, cousin, who officiated at the service and in the same breath he said that Smellie had run off as there was some scandal afoot. Though I could tell he was on the verge of exploding with wishing to tell me all, for his lips they did quiver much, I knew at once that if I wished to get the true facts, I would have to appeal to yourself, for as much as I admire my neighbour, he has sent me off on many a wild goose chase with inaccuracies and exaggerations, bless his kind soul.

So please, cousin, write back when you get an opportunity and tell me if you have been reinstated as a favourite with Lady Catherine (so that I may sleep soundly at night, knowing that my departure from this world is not an event which will be celebrated far and wide) and tell me, in truth, what did become of this not-so-reverend Smellie.

In anticipation and with kind regards to Thomas, Richard and Charlotte (who I believe is with child again so the heartiest of congratulations from all the Bennets. You are fast catching up with us, sir, and if you continue at this speed shall soon be blessed with a dozen little Collinses').

Yours sincerely,

Henry Bennet

Hunsford,
near Westerham,
Kent.

15th September, 1795

Dear Sir,

Please pardon my absent-mindedness for it had never dawned on me that my last letter would not reach you before your departure to the Bingleys'. I did find it strange that you had not responded to comfort me in my hour of need and feared that the comments therein referring to your own estate may have angered you against us, for Charlotte and I are in no hurry to take over the Longbourn Estate, just yet.

Although we are due to visit Lucas Lodge next month, I am content to put information your way to satisfy your impatience and curiosity, with regard to the irregular circumstances leading up to the wedding of July 18th, as I know you to be a man of indisputable discretion and integrity. I implore you however, sir, to keep the contents of this letter absolutely secret and would go so far as to encourage you to destroy it upon reading, that its contents should never be generally known to any but you and certainly not made public.

Such a furore as descended upon us in the week of the wedding, I shall never forget. During their stay, I had met Lord and Lady Smock and Mr Harold Smock several times, for when they were not at Rosings they very generously condescended to call on us at the parsonage, the honour of which alarmed and delighted us, for we had been very much cast into the shadows up to this point which troubled me *greatly. Charlotte declared Mr Smock to be a very pleasant young man and felt he was too superior of personality and mind for Miss Anne de Bourgh. This surprised me greatly and caused me to repudiate, for he spoke of Miss de Bourgh with fondness and looked forward with great enthusiasm to his wedding day and I doubted not but that his passion was reciprocated. And how Charlotte could forget that she too was once all infatuation and zealousness with regards a certain union, I know not how she failed to see it in others, for who could hear Mr Smock's declaration that his betrothed was as beautiful as the Atrophaneura Hector and as light as the Polygonia Comma and be unmoved? Though he be a peculiar looking gentleman, his superior breeding and impeccable dress more than make up for any lack in his appearance and cannot have gone unnoticed by his bride-to-be. But as I was to have no intimate involvement in the wedding preparations, everything to do with it and every mention of it pained me greatly and I returned each afternoon with a heavy heart to my troublesome vegetable patch that I might lose myself in its therapeutic gifts.*

On the morning before the wedding day, there came such a knock and thundering bang on my door at dawn that woke the entire household. It was one of the servants from Rosings, shouting out my name: "Mr Collins, come at once. You are needed at Rosings." It did not require a second airing; within minutes I was attired and departing for Rosings with the boy who knew not the nature of the business, and I feared that some terrible affliction had fallen upon Lady Catherine. On reaching Rosings, I was ushered into the breakfast room where Lady Catherine sat, quite pale, in the company of Mrs Jenkinson who stood up and rushed from the room crying as I entered. I fell to my knees beside her ladyship and begged to know that she was quite well. "Arise at once, Mr Collins, from *that hideous position and pull yourself together that you can be of some assistance to me,*" *she ordered and proceeded to tell me that she had just been informed by Mrs Jenkinson that Miss Anne de Bourgh was planning to elope with the Reverend Smellie that very afternoon.*

I had to sit immediately, without waiting for permission from my hostess, for my legs did shake with the shock of the news I had just received. Fortunately, Lady Catherine was not consulting me for advice, for she has wisdom enough for both of us, but looking for me to conspire with her as follows: Mrs Jenkinson, whom Lady Catherine dismissed the moment she came to raise the alarm, was to be sent off immediately to town to visit her sister and receive a handsome payment in return for her silence, including a generous annuity. Miss Anne de Bourgh was locked into her room where Lady Catherine would deal with her later and where she was to remain imprisoned until the wedding service on the morrow. I was assigned the post of accompanying Lord, Lady and Mr Smock on a trip to Maidstone for the supposed purpose of collecting the ancestral jewels from Lady Catherine's banker, a job I was to convince Mr Smock would win him great favour with his bride-to-be. Meanwhile, as I kept the visitors out of her way, her ladyship would descend upon the inn at which Miss de Bourgh was to meet Reverend Smellie at the appointed time and deal with him there.

This last point horrified me and I begged Lady Catherine to allow me to accompany her on this crusade that I might protect her in the event that some ugly business might transpire. I made reference to my boxing skills (for I did study with Daniel Mendoza, boxing champion and author of The Art of Boxing 1789 *before he became serious in the sport) at which she snorted and told me not to be ridiculous. There was no need for witnesses, she said, and she was well capable of dealing with Smellie in her own manner, for she had been the recipient of the greatest betrayal and he would feel the full force of her vengeance. All this alarmed me greatly and made any disapproval I had received from her in the past pale in comparison to what I now witnessed, but as I was swept up in the weight and urgency of my assignment I had not time to lose. Calling upon St. Michael, Archangel, the great warrior and protector, who did cast Satan down to the fires of Hell, I took one last fleeting look at her ladyship and began immediately about my mission.*

We returned late from Maidstone and I could hardly recall how the day was spent for my mind was elsewhere, though I believe I must have displayed unusual behaviour for Lord Smock did enquire, on several occasions, if I felt quite well. I returned to dress at the parsonage before moving at speed to Rosings to join the other guests for dinner but in particular to ensure she, whose safety and life I had feared for, was well.

When I arrived at Rosings, not only did I find no fright or confusion but, with the exception of Miss Anne de Bourgh being absent under the pretence of resting for her 'big day', I discovered Lady Catherine to be in the best spirits I had seen in many years. She made no reference to her meeting with Smellie with the exception of announcing during dinner that the Reverend Smellie had left Rosings that morning due to business of the most urgent nature that could not be delayed. She informed all that he sent his sincere apologies to the wedding party but felt extremely confident that Mr Collins would officiate wonderfully for he had such great passages written for the occasion that could not be compared with. This appeared to satisfy the guests who at first appeared shocked and concerned but then on being reassured that I would step in at their hour of need, were completely at ease and never ceased expressing their gratitude all evening. In their eyes, a calamity had been averted (little did they know that they were fortunate not to be missing a bride as well as a celebrant).

The wedding itself went particularly well and without interruption – if there were anyone present displeased with it (or with my wonderful passages) it entirely escaped me for I was quite in my element. The happy couple are to reside at Rosings in the company of Lady Catherine, that she may watch over them and assist them in the early days of wedded bliss.

We have heard nothing of the whereabouts of Reverend Smellie save that there is a rumour afoot, in ecumenical circles, that he has moved to Scotland, but I cannot confirm this as true.

So there, cousin, you find the delicate particulars which I know you will not share with your beloved; though I know she would be most discreet, I would prefer if temptation to talk on this matter (with her sister Philips in Meryton or others) would not be presented to Mrs Bennet, that she should not have to battle with her conscience, and again, I ask you, sir, to please destroy this letter on reading.

We look forward to meeting you all mid-October and introducin you to Richard.

In confidence and trust, your cousin,

William Collins

Longbourn,
near Meryton,
Hertfordshire.

27th September, 1795

Dear Sir,

I wish to thank you most heartily for your thorough explanation of the events leading to my confusion of late regarding nuptials and disappearing reverends. It now stands as one of my favourite correspondences from Kent and I will be sure to destroy it, I am sure, when I think of it but not before I commit its contents to my memory.

I am reassured on three points – firstly that you have been reappointed the resident ecumenical master of Rosings, thereby reducing my need to move onto my heavenly home just yet. Secondly, that the Reverend Smellie has disappeared, we are to assume, into the Highlands where we know he will get a few swift and hard belts of a highland targe across the back of the head if he attempts any of his trickery in their company. Thirdly, that the former Miss Anne de Bourgh is every bit as silly as Miss Lydia Bennet had once been, proving yet again, that in matters of the heart, the rich, as well as the poor, can make insipidly stupid mistakes. It would appear that Lady Catherine and I have more parental scrapes in common than we either of us had ever appreciated, all the more to foster empathy and understanding between us.

I am most troubled on behalf of our noble Mr Smock (and I ne'er get distressed on behalf of another person, rarely doing so for myself) that such a double-crossing were hatched against him by that rascal Smellie who, it would appear, was not satisfied with setting his sights on a humble parsonage but on Rosings Park itself. Lady Catherine must be on her guard in future about whom she invites into her home, for had Smellie not become accustomed to her fine port and carving meats at the head of her Louis XIV dining table, I am convinced he would have been less tempted to elevate himself so greatly in his own opinion and make come-hither eyes at her daughter. Evidently, he acquired a taste for upper gentry living and found that it was quite to his liking.

Praise the Lord it has all ended well but I cannot help but wonder if the new Mrs Smock is quite satisfied that her plans were foiled. I do hope she learns to appreciate the very great man she has married and that they may have a delightful life together.

We very much look forward to seeing you all in the coming weeks. Mrs Bennet is quite lonesome and loves the noise of children running about, a most unusual trait for a sufferer of headaches. I myself am looking forward to meeting young Thomas again and introducing him to the piglets.

Your cousin,

Henry Bennet

Hunsford,
near Westerham,
Kent.

9th November, 1795

Dear Sir,

On behalf of Charlotte, Thomas, Richard and my good self, may I thank you most heartily for the kindness which we were in receipt of on our many visits to Longbourn over the last number of weeks and that we met with the Darcys several times at your home was most fortuitous. Charlotte was overjoyed to spend so much time with Elizabeth and the children and Thomas, asks for you every day since our return.

I have just arrived now from Rosings where all is joy and happiness and pass on the regards of all within who listened with the utmost interest to my retelling of our delightful days spent in Hertfordshire. You will be relieved to hear that Lady Catherine did not once enquire after your health but was most persistent in learning who the current tenants of Netherfield Hall might be. She said she was making enquiries on behalf of an acquaintance and that she would contact the agent directly herself that she may be informed as soon as the lease became available. I am also delighted to report that, according to her ladyship, the married couple are very attached to each other although Mrs Smock likes to keep very separate arrangements from her husband and naturally, due to her ill-health (as well as his) and a reluctance to leave the stuff of youth behind, a period of transition is to be expected.

Due to the tumultuous year I have had to endure, my poor

vegetable patch did suffer much and provided us with merely a handful of turnips, carrots and fennel but thankfully, as we are now regular visitors at Rosings, our crop was surplus to requirements.

I have little else to add for all has returned to the quiet and serenity of previous years, where little happens in our humble lives, and we thank God for it. I am truly blessed and when I look upon Charlotte in her current situation of expectancy and my two darling boys, may I wish all at Longbourn equal peace all the days of their lives.

In gratitude and appreciation, your cousin,

William Collins

Longbourn,
near Meryton,
Hertfordshire.

18th December, 1795

Dear Sir,

I have just now re-read your last correspondence of six weeks hence that I might recall what were our pressing issues and respond as appropriate, to find that its tone was one of complete harmony and gratitude. And what more can we ask for, sir, as Christmas approaches than such an attitude and a deep appreciation for one's blessings?

We are all well here, excepting Mary whom I found quite unwell this morning, doubled over in what appeared to be agonies. She is so private in her business that I fear she often goes neglected so I was alarmed to see such a demonstration of debilitation and insisted I call for the physician but she refused and said she would be well again. Recommending the therapeutic benefits of a hot bath, I kept a distant eye and she does appear to have regained her health this evening. I believe, sir, she reads and thinks too much and should spend more time outdoors or playing music. There is a depth to Mary that few but I appreciate.

We enjoyed seeing you all of late in our native land and Master Thomas, in particular, is always welcome at the Longbourn estate for I did find in him such an accomplice in mischief that brought me back many decades. There is more Bennet than either Collins or Lucas in that boy for he helped me make a cross-bow and caught one of the hens with such skill as left me dumbfounded and reminded me of nobody more than myself. Please send him my special regards and tell him that the cat has returned but without his tail.

On other matters, we had the new school master come to dine last evening and I find him not one bit offensive, which surprised me greatly, for I generally like to fall out with educators due to their conservatism and fondness for the high moral ground. It confirms what I had come to note when observing myself of late – that I am becoming more and more mellow in my old age. Mrs Bennet tells everyone that there is no difference between how I or Shep, our sheepdog, react when she is relating a tale of great concern, for I consistently fail to panic, even slightly, when there is ample excuse for hysteria.

But back to this new school master, Mr Jenkins, a likeable chap (with a handsome face, according to Mrs B) and a great brain. I am pleased for the local families that he will take their offspring in hand for he teaches from the great Dutchman, Martinet's, works which state that one must study nature if one is to understand God's design. We had quite a great deal to discuss about Martinet's *Kort begrip der waereld-histoire voor de jeugd* (Brief Understanding of World-History for the Young). Would that such material were in circulation back in my day!

He came in the company of a Mr Luther who, despite his promising name, declares he has not a religious bone in his body, being a man of science. I must warn you, for he will be one of your closest neighbours someday, that he is considered with great suspicion in these parts, having killed many of his own livestock by accidentally mixing up a medicinal bottle with one of his home-made potions. Only this new Mr Jenkins and I seem to find him an interesting chap; all others fear that he will pour a poison in the wells and kill us all. Mrs Bennet swore she would not let him near the sauce boat and refused to touch it herself once she saw he had use of it before her.

Mr Jenkins' own situation, however, is to be pitied for his wife, Diane, is an invalid and remains in London (Cheapside, like the Gardiners) where her sister cares for her while he must needs take work where he can find it. I do sincerely hope that this does not mean that he will disappear again soon once a position closer to London materialises. I should not have mentioned the Gardiners, however, for I fear I may have embarrassed him somewhat (for he jumped when I mentioned Cheapside) as their circumstances must be hard-pressed and perhaps they do not socialise in the same circles or with the same frequency as the jovial, outgoing Gardiners.

Otherwise, we are readying ourselves for Christmas for, yet again, like a bad head-cold, it comes upon us suddenly when we seem to least expect it, similar to the Wickhams, who are to join us this festive season. Mrs Bennet is delighted (for she enjoys the noise), Mary is infuriated (for she hates it) and I am indifferent for my hearing loss has accelerated and I find the ailment suits me considerably.

May I wish you, Charlotte and the boys as well as all at Rosings the most wonderful of Christmases and New Year.

Sincere wishes,

Henry Bennet

1796 — The year in which a soldier becomes a sailor, a bachelor becomes a widower and we lose a loved one.

Hunsford,
near Westerham,
Kent.

12th January, 1796

Dear Sir,

Wishing all at Longbourn the happiest of New Years. May God's mercy and blessings descend upon you all, even those who stay with you at present.

While I have absolutely no inclination to ever become acquainted with the unchristian Mr Luther, I was most interested to learn of your new teacher, Mr Jenkins, but I would like to caution you, cousin, not to be so readily impressed by this foreign writer Martinet of whom I know little. For what can he write and teach our young about morals and the many evil temptations that exist today that cannot be better learnt directly from God's own word in the Good Book? And as a man of the outdoors myself, who appreciates nature like few others, I have to warn you that nature can oft lead man to sin and lose his soul for all eternity – a devil in angel clothing, one might say.

I tell you now, sir, of such an occurrence which I witnessed last week, in the most guarded language, that I may not sully your untainted mind. I happened to call upon a neighbouring farm to find my gardener John, who does oft work for them during the winter, to have a word regarding removing the dead ivy from the garden wall, when I was instructed I would find him in the barn. There I was met with such a sight that it were many moments before I could decipher there were two persons before me. Suffice to say the servant girl was present, as was John, neither were attired and I could not make sense of what I saw for I had never witnessed such an act, nor thought it possible, that I did that evening resort to Reverend Smellie's book, confident that I would discover it within. I believe I have narrowed it down to be either the act found on page 772 or that found on page 858.

I will mention no more, sir, but suffice to say there was such a sermon about carnal desires that Sunday which left the sinners in no doubt that they are destined for the fires of hell. Following much shuffling and coughing, not one eye could meet mine as the congregation left the church and even my own Charlotte did not speak to me for two days. And, therefore, I warn you now that while God did create nature and has dominion over all the land, the seas and creatures of this world, He will show no mercy to those who are not pure of spirit but wanton in their nature and use of nature. Forgive me again for mentioning this unclean subject to you, who like me is of an innocent disposition and not to be tempted by base inclinations, but I feel satisfied that nothing less would suffice in warning you to be careful of what you are about, particularly when young and innocent minds are at risk.

Your mention of Cheapside in your last letter planted a most ingenious idea in my head. I believe I shall call upon the Gardiners when I am in town next month, for I recall you stated, when we were last in Hertfordshire, that they will visit you at Easter and I have many books for the library at Longbourn which I would like them to deliver to you. As we expect our next blessing before then, it may be some time before we venture into Hertfordshire ourselves so I would be most grateful and indebted if they would perform this kindness for me and will send them a note this very evening, informing them of my intention.

Finally, I wish to say that all is not as one would wish at Rosings as there seems to be a marked change of tone in young Mr Smock towards her ladyship which concerns me greatly. Charlotte tells me it has been like this for several months but I fear I had not noticed as I cannot imagine that any person would present hostility to such a generous, noble hostess. And though I had always believed the young couple were attached, Charlotte again informs me that I was in error and that Mrs Smock despised her husband for the first many months of their union. Now, however, Mr and Mrs Smock are inseparable and entirely besotted due, according to my dear wife, to the very fact that Mr Smock rebels against her ladyship. I hope that this phase will pass and he will return to a more humble and grateful disposition soon for I am all awkward and uneasiness when dining at Rosings of late.

My very best, again, to you, Mrs Bennet, Mary and your visitors for '96.

Yours sincerely,

William Collins

Longbourn,
near Meryton,
Hertfordshire.

3rd March, 1796

Dear Sir,

Our heartiest congratulations to your good self and Charlotte on welcoming a wonderful daughter, Louisa, into the world. The very late Sir Lewis de Bourgh must be the most fortunate of departed souls to feature in all three of your progeny's names and I dare say the former Miss Anne de Bourgh has some catching up to do (although I have heard from Sir William Lucas that she has made a start and will be welcoming a little Smocklet in due course). I am sure that the arrival of a grandchild will soften all relations at Rosings, if they are indeed still fraught, as all inhabitants unite in their doting over the next generation.

There is little news here. Mary commenced presenting piano lessons at the school last month (for she has a charitable spirit) though it took considerable encouragement on my part but I persevered and she finally acceded. Perhaps she reads too many ecumenical writings for she is a troubled soul who I hear walking about her room at night. I believe that her health will benefit greatly from the short journey to the school and back and by engaging her mind through teaching and talking with others outside of these walls. The school, through Mr Jenkins' efforts, had recently received a donation of the old piano from Netherfield Hall when the current tenants purchased a new one. Which puts me in mind of that peculiar business of Lady

Catherine making enquiries regarding its current occupants. I do so hope she is not considering taking up residence at Netherfield herself, for although she is mild-mannered and benevolent and would be a most wonderful neighbour, she had best set her sights elsewhere for we have it from the current tenants, Colonel and Mrs Lacey, that they are here to stay. Console her ladyship as best you can and advise her that the summers are much warmer in Kent so she had best stay where she is.

The Gardiners, whom you recently visited with your shipment of books, are due to arrive within the fortnight and will be taking the boy, George Wickham Junior, with them when they return to town. There he will be reunited with his parents, for they left him here last month as they returned to friends in town. I cannot tell you what a joy it has been to have him here (and without them) and he shows great promise if his environment is steady and encouraging. It pains me to think how things may turn out for him for now his father, in a peacock display of bravado, declares that he is turning to the sea and joining the war against the French. I fear his real motive is that he has burnt many bridges and made many enemies on land and has little choice but to turn to the sea. Howsoever, we will enjoy every minute with our grandson and try to console and distract ourselves by visiting the other grandchildren when he has left.

Finally, sir, I would like to discreetly mention that occurrence in your neighbour's barn which threw you into a state of discomposure. Your caution is very much appreciated and your relating such a sensitive subject with such discretion and delicacy is an art-form in, and of, itself and one for which I must commend you. However, sir, never consider that you have to keep such happenings to yourself in future. Unburden yourself at once, cousin, and lay out the details to me in any manner you see fit for it must have weighed heavily on your mind, keeping this troublesome business secret from the very respectable company you keep. For have I not often observed to my girls, when we come across that passage in the bible regarding being as innocent as a child in order to enter the kingdom of Heaven, that such is the mind of Mr Collins – "a mind as innocent and empty now as it was on the very day that his mother brought him forth into this wicked world." So please feel free to lay out all the details of such mischievousness before me that I may learn from the wicked and base.

My library looks forward to your books, for there are several shelves down low, behind the door, which have remained empty for generations and will appreciate being occupied at last.

Your cousin,

Henry Bennet

Hunsford,
near Westerham,
Kent.

11ᵗʰ April, 1796

My Dear Sir,

May I take this opportunity to thank you most heartily for your kind wishes on the safe arrival of Louisa into our happy home and confirm that all are well, praise the Lord. We expect Charlotte's parents, as per usual, in the coming weeks. I am afraid, however, that Lady Catherine took exception to the fact that we have named our girl 'Louisa' for she believes it the most fitting name for her grandchild, be it born a girl, therefore, in her opinion, we have stolen it without asking prior permission. It was too late when we learned of her displeasure and, therefore, we cannot rename the child now and I wait with trepidation and pray that the Smocks welcome a boy.

I am most glad to hear you are keeping vigilant with regards Mary's health but, pray, do not discourage her enthusiasm for ecumenical studies for one's soul is ever more important than one's flesh. Fortunately, I have included in the case of books which should be, even now, making their way to you, via the Gardiners, such a variety of new interpretations and sermons based on the Good Book as cannot lead her astray and will lighten her spirit with renewed vigour and praise, for I believe a lack of good reading material is all that ailed her from the start.

I am indifferent to the news that Mr Wickham is to be sent to sea, for the Lord will find him out wherever he may be, but I do pray for the young boy's soul, that it shall be kept on the right path and not on the evil one which seemed to be preordained for him.

Our very best wishes to all at Longbourn.

Your devoted cousin,

William Collins

Longbourn,
near Meryton,
Hertfordshire.

5th May, 1796

Dear Sir,

I found your previous correspondence so full of the wrath of God that it did make me wonder whether perhaps it was the wrath of Lady Catherine that did colour the ink on your quill, however, as I have learned that she did indeed welcome a grandson into the world, Lewis Richard Edmund Smock, I imagine charity and forgiveness has returned to the world once more.

We received the Gardiners and your books into the house at Easter, only parting with them last Wednesday (the Gardiners, not your books) and, I must say, it was a jolly few weeks. Mr Jenkins, the school master, joined us many times during their stay and, I must confess, his mind is a great one. I have rarely met one as good (excepting yourself of course, cousin). He also kindly helped me rearrange all books in the library and even wrote a catalogue that I may never lose a map or pamphlet again. There appears to be a depth of soul to him, that I believe is not revealed often or to many, but I would place a wager on his writing poetry in private. I did find that he became excessively embarrassed when Mr Gardiner engaged him on his acquaintance and whereabouts in Cheapside which confirms my theory that his manner of living contrasts greatly with that of the Gardiners. I imagine whatever he feels, he feels deeply.

Of course, I miss young George Wickham very much now that he has left but a letter from Lydia telling me that she intends to join us at the Bingleys' fine home in the coming weeks has put my mind at ease.

Mary's spirits appear good in the mornings and failing in the afternoons. I continue to be vigilant that she eats sufficiently, however, she refuses to see a physician, despite one calling frequently to the house to visit Mrs Bennet and her many complaints. A trip to the Bingleys and Darcys shall do her the world of good, though she cried when I told her. I thought it a good time to hint that I was aware that a beautiful soul such as she could not always be kept in big houses in England, for I do not wish guilt or anxiety for the future to add to her troubles. She kissed me on the forehead and said that I loved her well and understood her greatly and seemed comforted by my words. We leave mid-May and will be back mid-June and perhaps we should be fortunate to meet with you all if you are planning a trip to Lucas Lodge this year.

Your cousin,

Henry Bennet

Hunsford,
near Westerham,
Kent.

16ᵗʰ June, 1796

Dear Sir,

I write to you now that I may reach you shortly after your return into the glorious Hertfordshire countryside. I pray that your trip was safe and that you found all my dear cousins and their families in the best of health and happiness on your visit to Derbyshire.

We are now planning a trip to stay at Lucas Lodge in early August, a most spontaneous decision, and have even more exciting news to impart – we will be joined for some small share of our time by Lady Catherine de Bourgh. Netherfield Hall has become vacant during your absence and her ladyship plans to inspect it – the current tenants, according to her ladyship's source, up and left very suddenly with little time for farewells due to the urgency of their business elsewhere. I did press her for more details, for I think it a strange business, but she frowned so disapprovingly upon me that I knew I must say no more on the subject. I flatter myself that her ladyship is perhaps looking ahead, at this juncture of her life, to settle close to where she knows will eventually be my permanent home though, may I repeat myself here, cousin, we are in no haste to acquire Longbourn just yet.

Yours sincerely,

William Collins

Longbourn,
near Meryton,
Hertfordshire.

20th July, 1796

Dear Sir,

The world has gone mad! Mr Collins, I have such a tale to tell you.

On our return last month, we were met on the very first evening by Mr Jenkins who practically invited himself to dinner and told us the very tragic news that his wife, Diane, was dying. We were saddened to hear it and, I must confess, my first thoughts were whether he would return into Hertfordshire and continue his work, as I had grown fond of the man, or whether he would be freer after her passing to move wherever he wished. May the Lord forgive my selfish thoughts when I should have been thinking of his heartbreak and worry. He was very glum that evening and was leaving for London the following morning.

Knowing that what lay ahead for him would be a painful, drawn-out business and considering he may be very many weeks without a salary, I decided in the morning to write to my brother-in-law Gardiner and request that he might drop in on the young man and offer his assistance, for he is well-connected in town. I knew that he did not have his exact address but knew the street on which he lived and would, therefore, be of much greater use than I could be in Longbourn.

The response I received back, the following week, was as follows: that Mr Gardiner eventually found Mr Jenkins' former residence (where he had lived until moving into our locality eight months ago) but that he had lived there alone and had never been wed. He confirmed this account with the store downstairs where Mr Jenkins had an account – there was never a wife, only a man in single lodgings.

I could not imagine what this was about and wondered what other lies this young man had told us and whether he had stolen something valuable from the school or elsewhere and perhaps had made good his escape. But who to tell and what to tell, I could not think, for I had nothing to accuse him of and, therefore, decided to say naught for another week or two to see if the blackguard would return.

And return Mr Jenkins did, the following Monday evening, in full mourning attire! You can imagine my alarm, for I did not know what to say as I watched all others sympathise with him. I beckoned him into my library after dinner and interrogated him there, showing him Mr Gardiner's letter and demanding a full explanation of events.

It transpired that Mr Jenkins was completely and utterly in love with Mary and had been from the first evening they had met here for dinner. But as he was accustomed to being deemed an eligible bachelor in every town he worked, causing two widows to get into quite a scrape over him at his last place of work, he swore that when he took up another post he would pretend that he was a married man. I was in a stunned silence, which he interpreted as permission to talk, so on he spoke. He had been torn in agonies. Even if he disclosed the fact that he was a bachelor, Mary had confided in him, early on, her secret plan to join a convent in Spain once I depart this world. But he was convinced that Mary and he were like two tuning forks vibrating on the same note. He had felt his "own heart beating within her ribcage". I requested he stop at this point for his language was becoming ungentlemanly and besides, to my mind, our practical Mary, unaware of his feelings, would think him quite mad. But he pressed on and asked me for her hand in marriage once he took up a new post which had become vacant as master at the large school in Meryton. He also had a moderate income from a small farm which he leased out in the south of the county that an uncle had left him. I conceded that if Mary wished to have him and loved him, I would content myself, then I asked him to wait in the front room while I spoke with her.

Mary, my sensible Mary, whom I believed I knew all of her life, began to shake and cry on hearing the news I disclosed. She confessed that on meeting Mr Jenkins that first night she felt an upheaval of emotions, an unearthly belonging. This was the reason, she told me, I had discovered her in such a state the following morning – sick at the thought that she would never have him and guilty that she even wished it.

Her delight in hearing that Mr Jenkins wished to marry her was truly moving and when I reunited the two, their genuine devotion, kept hidden so long from each other, poured forth until I felt I was imprisoned in a novel of some sort. These young people are so passionate nowadays that I wonder what ever became of smiling at a girl across a ball room and securing her affection with a dance.

I will bore you no more, cousin, with the tale of two young lovers, for I know how deeply you once felt it yourself, but suffice to say that the absence of neither long walks nor long sermons were at the root of Mary's ailment and, it would appear, that only love could cure it.

I have not room, mental or on paper, for to tell you much else other than Mrs Bennet has not smelling salts enough to support her through the shock she has just received and I only regret now that I had not placed a wager on Mary becoming wed one day.

Our love to all at Hunsford and we look forward to meeting you (and Lady Catherine) in August.

Your affectionate cousin,

Henry Bennet

Lucas Lodge.

9th August, 1796

We are come, dear cousin, we are come!

Sir William and Lady Lucas have requested that I include in this note (announcing our safe arrival into the glorious Hertfordshire countryside) an invitation for you all to dine with us tomorrow evening at Lucas Lodge for my sister-in-law, Maria Lucas, is just now engaged to Captain McCarthy and we wish you to join in our celebration of the good news.

I look forward to our meeting for I found your last letter most lacking in useful information, choosing instead to go into far too great detail with regards the emotions of one young couple. And although few, and Charlotte may vouch for this, understand the burning fire of love and the depths of fervency as I do, you must remember, sir, that they were acting in a most improper and sinful way to hold passionate, nay, lustful thoughts about the other while the pretence of Mr Jenkins being married was believed to be true: James 1:15 "… after desire is conceived, it gives birth to sin …" I am most alarmed at Mary. You certainly encouraged vice and were I you, I would have punished them both most severely but, on mature consideration, what is one to expect from a man who teaches that nature is of greater importance and standing than the word of God?

I would have much preferred to have learned from your letter (rather than hearing it from another source) that both Mr Darcy and Mr Bingley were asked to run for parliament, that Mr Gardiner has closed a most lucrative deal with the admiralty and that your grandson George Wickham Junior is to come live with you from Michaelmas to Christmas.

I look forward with great enthusiasm to seeing you on the morrow that we may discuss the arrival of Lady Catherine de Bourgh into the county for to inspect Netherfield Hall and how best to impress her while here. I expect a letter by tomorrow's post for she has promised to write to inform me of her itinerary and plans for Hertfordshire.

Yours sincerely,

William Collins

Longbourn.

10th August, 1796

Dear Cousin,

We would be delighted to join all the Lucases for dinner this evening and to celebrate Maria's engagement to an outstanding man, Captain McCarthy (whom I once witnessed gargle 'God Save the King' with the most astonishing clarity). We had heard the happy news in the first instance from my sister-in-law Philips who dropped in last week to inform us, in her usual thunderous tone, of the engagement some three days before the couple in question had come to an understanding and got down on one knee etcetera.

Let me satisfy your curiosity regarding the news items you referred to in your note, Darcy immediately refused to run for parliament, being too sensible for such tomfoolery, while Bingley, not wishing to disappoint anyone, toyed with the idea, but when, following an interview with the man, the powers-that-be found him too liberal and indecisive, they retreated with speed and denied any knowledge of having ever asked him to step forward (much to his relief).

Mr Gardiner, it is true, has tripled his purse and deserves every bit of good fortune that comes his way and young George is indeed due to join us while his mother pretends to wait anxiously in town for news from her negligent, seafaring husband.

By the by, the hapless Mr Luther, our local man of science, whom I mentioned to you before, was pulled out of the river last night by poachers. It would appear that he was trying to gather frogs for experimentation but lost his footing. Fortunately for him, he lives, but, unfortunately, he told the poachers the nature of his experiment (namely creating a poison which kills insects and small rodents) which only increases fear and paranoia in the surrounding community. I daresay they wished they had left him where he was and were tempted to have him lose his footing once more.

Finally, I am happy to discuss the imminent arrival of Lady Catherine but I must warn you that, as she is not my patroness, I am under no obligation to make a spectacle of myself on her behalf, but she is welcome to join me in my library any evening, given due notice, and I may even open a good bottle of port in her honour.

Until this evening,

Henry Bennet

Postscript – There was something in today's *Gazette* regarding your old friend, the Reverend Smellie. Apparently, he was caught in the possession of a number of artefacts of considerable value which were stolen from a great house in Cheshire last year. I shall bring the *Gazette*, that we may discuss the latest intrigues of Smellie.

Longbourn.

15th August, 1796

Dear Sir,

I send you this brief note as I tried to gain admittance to Lucas Lodge earlier to see how you fare but I was informed that you are still indisposed. I believe Charlotte thinks it my fault.

But was it not a marvellous trick?

And I have no doubt that had you not the larger share of a bottle of cognac in you at the time, you would not have seen it through! I admire you, sir, for taking a dare which risked the displeasure of your noble patroness but you did it, cousin, you pulled it off. Imagine the look on her face when she finds her horses hitched toward her carriage instead of facing away … and if you were not in fits of laughter before the fall, perhaps we might have had the pleasure of witnessing her reaction from a safe hiding-place but, alas, it was not to be.

In all solemnity, we were not to know that there was an eight-foot drop on the other side of that hedge, but your head, it will heal, as they are making such a fuss of you at Lucas Lodge. And were we not extremely fortunate that Baroness Herbert was charging past at just the right time to offer us a lift home?

Until you come to visit, when you are recovered, your secret is safe with me.

Henry Bennet

Hunsford,
near Westerham,
Kent.

25th August, 1796

Dear Sir,

I hope this letter finds all at Longbourn well this fine Autumnal day as I include the fondest wishes of my dear Charlotte who, having secured me back to Hunsford, has now softened in her approach to my relatives at Longbourn. You must allow, sir, that she was merely alarmed by my condition and worried for our future at Hunsford in the event of her ladyship ever discovering who was behind the practical joke. Mrs Collins' outright ban on any interaction between you and me for the reminder of our stay in Hertfordshire was precautionary only (for I did promise her that I would never consume liquor so early in the morning again).

And so, cousin, let us never make reference to the incident again for I am greatly ashamed of my conduct and must console myself that had I not been tempted, like the snake tempted Eve, I should never have sinned against Lady Catherine, whom I look up to with such reverence and to whom I owe so much.

I acted in a moment of deep and bitter disappointment on learning that she was purchasing Netherfield Hall, not for herself but for her daughter and son-in-law, for I was fully convinced that she would be loath to part from me someday. On mature reflection, however, she was acting, as usual, with the most selfless and noble of intentions, putting the health and happiness of her family first, for she has now halved the distance that they will have to travel to visit his family in Warwickshire and yet are a similar distance to Rosings. Meanwhile they will benefit from having connections in the locality through the Lucases and Bennets, to help them establish themselves (though it be inferior society but will suffice until introductions to the greater houses are made). And will not I, myself, one day be in a position to keep a watchful eye on them, on behalf of my patroness, when we move to Hertfordshire permanently?

You may have heard that Smellie (for I shall no longer call him reverend) has escaped custody and is believed to have returned to Scotland where his friends offer him refuge. I pray that he will be caught or escape abroad for he sends a shiver up and down my back when I think of him.

Thomas asks me to inform you that it was he who hid Mrs Hill's good apron and you will find it in the loft in the shed where you keep the pigs. I have reprimanded him for such conduct and would be grateful if you would inform Mrs Hill at your earliest convenience.

Your affectionate cousin,

William Collins

Longbourn,
near Meryton,
Hertfordshire.

20th September, 1796

Dear Sir,

May I wish you, and all at Hunsford, well as another busy harvest draws to a close for us here at Longbourn which, yet again, saw Sir William and myself demonstrate our unique dance arrangements in front of a large, amused and appreciative crowd of farm workers.

I am most pleased that Charlotte has bestowed her permission for us to communicate again and I acknowledge that what appears to be harmless frivolity in the eyes of one, is a grave impropriety in the eyes of another where reputations and patronage are concerned. Let her rest assured that her lamb shall not be led astray again, but I cannot guarantee that her son, Thomas, and I shall not rob a few plums from the trees at Lucas Lodge on his next sojourn.

I look forward with great enthusiasm to the arrival of the Smock family into Hertfordshire and Netherfield and hope to be one of the first gentlemen to call next Thursday fortnight when they arrive. And though our society might be 'inferior' for a time, I would be happy to introduce them to their grander neighbours, such as the carriage-driving Baroness Herbert.

And as eager as I am to make the acquaintance of Harold Smock and his butterflies, which I assume will be escorting him to Netherfield, I am even more thrilled to be reunited with young Georgie Wickham as he arrives to us around about the same time. His mother leaves him here until Christmas when she takes him back to London as she expects Lord Nelson and the French will call a truce to facilitate her husband getting home for a week or two.

I fear you may never meet with the great scientific mind that is Mr Luther if he continues as he does. Last week he succumbed to toxic fumes and collapsed at his home, only to be discovered by a passing farmer who, on hearing an explosion, ran into the house and dragged the unfortunate man out into the fresh air. The physician said he was lucky to be alive and may have caused immeasurable damage to his lungs.

I believe I heard that you are expected at Lucas Lodge for Christmas, staying until early January (when Maria Lucas is to wed), and the same informant has let slip that her ladyship comes to Netherfield at the same time to visit the Smocks. We shall have a jolly old time of it (minus the consumption of alcohol in the morning!).

Your sincere cousin,

Henry Bennet

Longbourn,
near Meryton,
Hertfordshire.

27th November, 1796

My Dear Sir,

On behalf of all the Bennet family, may I offer our deepest condolences to Charlotte, you and the children on the sudden but peaceful passing of our dear friend, Sir William.

His continuous good humour and kindness will be very greatly missed by us all here at Longbourn and in Meryton, where he maintained all his former friendships with a good-will and virtue that is rarely witnessed in this age:

"How blessed is the man to whom the Lord does not impute iniquity, and in whose spirit there is no deceit." Psalm 32:2

We understand that you cannot be here for the funeral ceremony but will arrive earlier at Christmas than you had originally planned. Let us know once you arrive that we may condole with you all in person. We will be sure to keep Lady Lucas company in her hour of sadness and increase our presence at Lucas Lodge in the coming months, and particularly once your family has returned to Kent, to ensure that she seldom finds herself lonesome (for she and Sir William were, as you know, extremely attached).

Your affectionate cousin,

Henry Bennet

Lucas Lodge.

19th December, 1796

Dear Sir,

We arrived at Lucas Lodge earlier this evening and, having spent many solemn hours comforting Lady Lucas in this time of great sorrow for all, we are now announcing our arrival and our hope that we may meet on the morrow. I have spent these last number of weeks, with great patience and humility, bringing together such passages from the Good Book as may be read to my mother-in-law each evening which will console and uplift her spirits.

As you are aware, my noble patroness, Lady Catherine de Bourgh, arrives at Netherfield Hall next week and I believe I do not speak in haste when I say that I expect an invitation to be extended to both Lucas Lodge and Longbourn during her stay.

Sincere good wishes until tomorrow,

William Collins

1797 — The year in which a sailor disappears, the deadly smallpox arrives and a great thief is compromised.

Longbourn,
near Meryton,
Hertfordshire.

27th January, 1797

Dear Sir,

I hope this letter finds you all (including her ladyship) back home safe and sound after your recent stay in Hertfordshire. We were glad to have you about as it was extra company and a distraction for Lady Lucas. And with Maria marrying the gargling-captain and leaving for Yorkshire, I have no doubt that your presence and passages were a great comfort. She did tell me that she particularly enjoyed the evening that we all dined together at Netherfield in the company of Lady Catherine, Baroness Herbert and the Smocks, remarking that if only Sir William were there he would have retold the story of how many years ago, at St James', His Royal Highness once mistook him for his former boot-boy.

And was it not marvellous that Lady Catherine and Baroness Herbert were already known to each other? Who would have thought that the latter had been a favourite with Sir Lewis de Bourgh, though she were seventeen years his senior? It is safe to surmise that their botched attempt at an elopement was hindered by the lady sitting at the top of the table and I believe Mr Harold Smock thought likewise for he gave me such a look as said "perhaps we should eat dinner with spoons, lest there be blood spilled." Though I dislike dining from home, in general, I did pass the most wonderful evening at Netherfield Hall.

Our alarming news, though I do not believe it to be true, is that George Wickham is missing at sea, presumed dead. A hysterical Lydia arrived in person to tell us as much. She and her mother are all in an uproar but the point is, it is not official so may only be hearsay. I have intervened by asking our son-in-law, Colonel Fitzwilliam, to make further enquiries with the admiralty so that quiet shall be restored to our house once more. Mary and I attempt to console and temper the pair but they think and talk of nothing else which does not surprise us.

Mary, as her wedding day approaches, is too much in love to care or expect a fuss to be made of her but, my, does she have a tranquil, blissful air about her. You would hardly know her, Mr Collins, from the solemn, bookish girl who rarely smiled and I daresay may not approve of her distracted air but as her father, I must be allowed to say, as the one I worried about most that, to know that a different life lies ahead for her gladdens my heart.

Your affectionate cousin,

Henry Bennet

Hunsford,
near Westerham,
Kent.

25th March, 1797

Dear Cousin,

We were in a most alarmed state, as you can imagine, sir, when word had yester-evening arrived at Hunsford that Mr Wickham has been discovered at last but is believed to be fatally wounded. Even as this letter makes its way to you now, he most likely has moved on from this life and so, as it is an almost certain event, may I extend our sincere sympathy to you all in this time of bereavement and upheaval for despite his being of low character, the good Lord has seen fit in his wisdom to take him to His breast now, that no more sin may come his way. And then a fitting judgement of his life shall take place by the only One who can see into the hearts and souls of men for whatever a man is sowing, he will also reap.

We think particularly of his son, George, who shall now, in remaining permanently at Longbourn, be shown the path of the righteous and it is, in the opinion of Charlotte, Lady Catherine and myself, a great blessing and a sign that the Lord has marked him as an innocent lamb who shall receive the generosity of His love and protection. Perhaps his mother, Lydia, will finally turn to the Lord for comfort and commence a quiet life of remorse and reflection.

May we also pass on our congratulations to Mary and Mr Jenkins on their recent marriage and apologise that we were not in attendance. We believe, as we received word from Lucas

Lodge, that it was an unadorned affair that did not attract much interest from local society and perhaps had I been requested to perform the ceremony, with my connection to Rosings and Netherfield Hall, that would not have been the case.

My noble patroness looks forward (with great excitement) to a visit from Mr and Mrs Smock in the coming weeks and what lively conversation and enjoyable times lie ahead for us during their sojourn. In the utmost confidence, sir, let me tell you that the distraction could not come at a better time, for her ladyship has just this week received a hideous letter, written anonymously, in an attempt to extract monies from her. She makes little of the matter and puts it down to the work of a roguish opportunist who knows not who he deals with.

Again, I wish to say that we are deeply concerned for you all during this trying time.

Your cousin,

William Collins

Longbourn,
near Meryton,
Hertfordshire.

6th April, 1797

Dear Sir,

May I wish you, Charlotte and all at Hunsford and Rosings a peaceful Easter. We thank you for you kind words on the passing of George Wickham and hope that he may find peace in the next world. The particulars of his injuries remain a mystery – what we do know is that he died from a gunshot wound but whether it were received during an act of mischief or heroism, we cannot ascertain.

And though I would have chosen different wording to that expressed in your last correspondence, we too are most grateful that young Georgie stays with us here at Longbourn. Mrs Bennet and he are particularly close and I notice that while she only showed a passing interest in her own children, she is positively obsessed with her grandchildren, constantly purchasing presents, rattles and bonny clothing. I am to speak with our brother Philips in Meryton to see how we proceed to take some legal steps to protect him here, for though his mother loves him dearly, she appears to be more content staying with friends in London and, although it is early days, she will, no doubt, set her sights on another husband before long as I fear a quiet life of remorse and reflection is no enticement for her.

Mary's wedding was a lovely affair and, if I do say so myself, my favourite of all five. There was simplicity about the service and a lack of fuss that saw the whole thing over and done with within the hour. Before I knew it, I was back at my library sipping a glass of malt and toasting my toes by the fire having waved the young couple off to their new lodgings in Meryton.

Georgie and I have planted a number of apple and pear trees, whose harvests will bear the Collins family more tarts and pies at some future date than their current owner, I fear, but such is my generous nature that it is of future generations I think!

Our very best to your family,

Henry Bennet

Postscript – I did bump into Mr Harold Smock the other day in Meryton and he was quite surprised at the level of excitement that awaits his visit to Rosings which I informed him of. He was more cautious in his hopes for the stay and implied that there is a learned man in Maidstone who claims to have discovered a rare breed of moth thereabouts, which is tempting him further south than he would otherwise have considered just now. I very near let slip about the anonymous letter but thinking that it could be a joke he, himself, was playing on her ladyship, I was very glad that I succeeded in keeping hush. I eagerly await his return that we may invite him to dine with us and talk over his adventures with our friends at Hunsford and Rosings.

Hunsford,
near Westerham,
Kent.

21ˢᵗ June, 1797

Dear Sir,

May I wish you all well and ask you to keep us in your prayers as our boy Thomas has been struck down with the pox. It has cruelly claimed six young lives in the village so far and we pray that the good Lord spares us our son.

My dear Charlotte is naturally distraught but stays with Thomas day and night and never sleeps. I now have the additional burden of fearing for her health, for what would become of us if we lost her too? We are none of us in our right senses during this stressful time. I was obliged to ask her ladyship to leave yester morn as she came into the house to give advice, recklessly endangering her own wellbeing and that of the Smocks by coming here. She naturally did not take kindly to being ordered to leave at once but I am sure when she reflects that it was for the best, she will forgive me in time.

As soon as we understood what we were contending with, we sent dear Richard and Louisa with their nurse to Lucas Lodge to ensure they are safe. I ask you now, cousin, to kindly offer your support to Lady Lucas who has this additional weight to carry in addition to her own grief.

In gratitude, your cousin,

William Collins

Longbourn,
near Meryton,
Hertfordshire.

24th June, 1797

Dear Sir,

Rest assured that we are lending our services to all at Lucas Lodge and wish to offer you any assistance you can think of. That young Thomas is in such danger and suffering so, breaks this old man's heart. Would that I could do anything for the boy or that it were me in his stead. Please tell him that I will not sell the piglets 'til he is here to come to market with Georgie and me.

We wait to hear from you.

You are all in our prayers.

Henry Bennet

Hunsford,
near Westerham,
Kent.

1st July, 1797

Dear Sir,

Our Thomas is safe, praise the Lord for his mercy, though we acknowledge that we have been fortunate where many have not and ask that you consider them in your prayers. I am joined by my dear Charlotte in thanking all at Longbourn for your attentiveness during our recent worry and in particular offering such kind assistance to your neighbour, Lady Lucas. Thomas now sits up in bed and his wounds are tended to by a local lady whom I have hired to take over now he is out of danger. Naturally, he is bored with his situation and wishes to be about – only the promise of a visit to Longbourn to sell the pigs at market with his cousin Mr Bennet can make an obedient patient of him, therefore, we may see you in September.

Although Charlotte is anxious to have Louisa and Richard back home, I have insisted that they do not return until she has had adequate time to recuperate and return to the full of her health for she has become so weakened by the past number of weeks that one would hardly recognise her as the same Charlotte.

Lady Catherine, in her limitless attentiveness, condescended to visit with us this morning in the company of Mrs Smock, both of whom displayed extreme compassion and in particular to my dear Charlotte. Nothing was said of our last encounter when I felt obliged to take on the role of *authority and request that her ladyship leave the premises. It is all forgot. They offered their services and insisted that we accept a visit from Lady Catherine's very own physician, Mr Wilkinson, who would have many useful lotions and advice regarding Thomas's wounds and at no cost to ourselves.*

Again, I thank you for your prayers and concern at this time. We are feeling blessed and grateful for our situation.

Your cousin,

William Collins

Longbourn,
near Meryton,
Hertfordshire.

6th July, 1797

My Dear Sir,

The relief Mrs Bennet, Georgie and I felt on reading your last correspondence cannot be surpassed. The happy fact that Thomas is out of danger can only be equalled by the fact that we will soon see him again, running about and shooting arrows at Longbourn. I have been cutting and seasoning a very good selection of lengths of wood for him for that very purpose while his dear old friend and occasional adversary, Mrs Hill, has promised to bake his favourite pies, bless her, she cried so on hearing he was safe.

We look forward to seeing you all in Hertfordshire in the not-too-distant future. Perhaps, if it coincides with your visit, you might do us the honour of stepping in on behalf of your late father-in-law, Sir William Lucas, at the harvest celebration, as he was a great favourite with our local folk. Though, I must warn you, that it is an occasion when you may have to leave etiquette at home for it is a far cry from the Netherfield ball but equally, if not more so, enjoyable.

The fondest of wishes to all your family,

Henry Bennet

Hunsford,
near Westerham,
Kent.

27th August, 1797

Dear Sir,

It is with the utmost delight that I wish to inform you that
the Collins family will be descending upon Lucas Lodge
on September 23rd for a fortnight stay and hope to see you
frequently during our visit. In particular, I believe I will be
present for the harvest festivities which you have planned for
early October (for a little bird has whispered in my ear that
is the expected time for completion of harvest) and only hope
that I will do justice to the memory of my late honourable
father-in-law. I have prepared a number of passages from the
Good Book which reference harvesting (of crop and souls) and
gratitude which I feel will be appreciated by those gathered,
prior to celebrations getting underway.

On a most serious note, Lady Catherine has, since my
last mention of the undesirable event, received a number of
letters of negative tone whose author appears to be the same
blackguard as before. She has now received five such letters
in total and continues to ignore them entirely, declaring that
they are the work of an opportunist and that in the course of
her work as magistrate she has drawn upon herself the spite of
many a detester of justice. I shall fret for her safety while we
are all in Hertfordshire and, therefore, recommended that she
consider inviting the Darcys or Fitzwilliamses to stay during
that time so that she would not be alone, but she would not

hear of it. I have ordered my man, John, to visit Rosings daily and keep a watchful eye out for any strangers lurking about the grounds.

We look forward to seeing you all in a number of weeks. Please pass on my fondest regards to all at Longbourn.

Your cousin,

William Collins

Hunsford,
near Westerham,
Kent.

15th October, 1797

Dear Mr Bennet,

Now that we have returned home to Hunsford parsonage, may I take this opportunity to formally express my regret once again for my conduct at your harvest festivities. Although I have sincerely apologised on every occasion that we met, I cannot help but blush at the remembrance of the particulars of that evening and recall to mind the integrity of the late Sir William Lucas and how I may have brought shame on his memory.

As I have stated time and again, the wonderful response I received to my passages from the workers present made me quite giddy and, as I had only partook of one cognac prior to my speech to assist with any agitation of mind, nerves or spirit, I am still at a loss as to how I became quite so inebriated thereafter. That I sprained an ankle while dancing and refused to quit has led to a very severe swelling that I have even yet as a daily reminder (and punishment) for my foolishness but that I returned home, at dawn, without my shirt is the point which both Charlotte and I find it most difficult to overcome.

It shames me to write this letter to you, cousin, but it is a shame that I will not attempt to avoid, for who but I should feel the full force of humiliation for behaving in such a heathen and disgraceful manner? Naturally, I have not disclosed this tale at Rosings, and though, unfortunately, many of the Netherfield staff were present, I would appreciate it if you would not mention it to Mr and Mrs Smock, unless they hear it elsewhere and you are compelled to tell some small discretionary untruth to cover over the horrible facts.

Pray, apologise on my behalf again to Mrs Hill, whose grandmother's trifle dish came to its demise by falling from my head.

By the by, Lady Catherine has received another anonymous letter this morning. Their tone is now quite threatening which only appears to please her ladyship and though I am glad to have returned to provide some protection at Rosings, she appears to neither wish it nor welcome it, so I must needs be subtle in my surveillance as I do not wish to displease my hostess.

I believe that I have discovered who the culprit is – none other than that sinister individual of old, Mr Bradford, who played so many tricks on my good character in the past. I have passed his home on several occasions ensuring that he noticed my presence on each occasion. When he finally asked me what I was about, I merely nodded at him that "I know that it is you." He stared blankly in response which is a sure indication of his guilt and remorselessness yet it should have been sufficient to put an end to his blackguarding.

Once more, regarding my recent conduct, cousin, I am forever in your debt for bearing with me and beg forgiveness again from the current master of Longbourn.

William Collins

Postscript – Forgive me for forgetting to enquire but I sincerely hope that your cough has passed. The vapours inhaled while taking a very warm bath can do your chest no end of good and, therefore, may I recommend it heartily.

Longbourn,
near Meryton,
Hertfordshire.

27th October, 1797

Dear Sir,

Please do not trouble yourself with further apologies. The whole business is quite forgot though, I am led to believe, it is still spoken about with great mirth amongst the clientele of The Lion's Head in the village ... a lively bunch, indeed, whom I am confident will forget it once an act of murder or madness catches their attention and, in these unsettling times, they will not have long to wait.

To speak the truth, I cannot comprehend why you are so severe upon yourself for, as a sober outsider looking in, you were merely having the most wonderful time and mixing with your flock in mutual appreciation of the Lord's bounty and blessings. Even Sir William Lucas, who presented with only a slightly milder form of antics to yourself, would be well pleased, from whatever heavenly perch he is observing, that your future neighbours, staff and farm labourers enjoyed your company to such a degree. It bodes very well for the future of the Longbourn estate.

Only Mrs Hill still holds some negative sentiment with regard to the trifle bowl but I successfully convinced her to put the past behind her and replace the bowl with something along a similar vein from the good china suppliers in Meryton. I enclose the bill that you may put her mind, and yours, at ease at your earliest convenience.

All at Longbourn enjoyed your recent stay immensely and it was marvellous to see young Thomas appear so well when one considers how truly sick he was. I hope that he enjoys my old box of soldiers. Georgie shows no interest in them whatsoever so it would greatly please this old man to pass them on to one who delights in them as much as I did, when little.

My cough has improved a little. Dear Mrs Bennet scolds me for attending the market in Meryton yesterday in heavy rainfall and though we joke and poke, how fond of each other we are! I reminded her that while the bullock is reputedly a wise creature, he has not yet worked out how to navigate his own way to town, sell himself and, in the same instance, return the abundant price he has fetched to the master and mistress of Longbourn; my dear wife owned that I had a point.

Mr Luther, our man of science, was pronounced dead last night. The physician found him slumped over his work desk, having been called by a concerned debt-collector. This Zacchaeus had discovered the body when he was leaving the premises through the kitchen window with a telescope beneath his arm and, conscientious man that he was, raised the alarm. Several minutes later, however, Mr Luther awoke, shouting "I have it!" and ran from the house. It is generally believed that, in the absence of rodents coming indoors this mild weather, he had been trying out his latest formulation on himself.

Finally, Sir, I would not worry about those anonymous letters if Lady Catherine does not. She is a lady of above average intelligence and cunning and if she is not stirred by a threat to her safety then perhaps there is none. Would she, perchance, have written those letters to herself as a joke to those in her company? I am sure it can be explained away in some light-hearted vein such as this.

Please pass on our fondest regards to all at Hunsford and Rosings.

Yours sincerely,

Henry Bennet

Hunsford,
near Westerham,
Kent.

16ᵗʰ December, 1797

My Dear Sir,

Before I impart details of a most alarming nature, let me commence by requesting that you extend the heartfelt good-will of the Collins family to all at Longbourn this Christmas and, in particular, as it is our understanding that you have many visitors this year, please be sure to wish each of my fair cousins and their families our very special and fondest regards.

Lady Lucas has informed us that the baby girl, Ellen, which was delivered to Mary and Mr Jenkins last month, so much earlier than anticipated, is a fine, strong, healthy child and in no way sickly or small. While this news has triggered gossip in some quarters, rest assured that we at Hunsford believe not a word of it and have said as much at Rosings despite her ladyship saying that "where the Bennet family are concerned, nothing would surprise me."

Now, however, cousin, I must prepare you for a most incredible shock. It has transpired that it was Smellie who wrote the threatening anonymous letters – he has been found and is back in prison but the circumstances which led to his capture are remarkable.

I was most alarmed and deeply concerned last Sunday evening that we were not invited to dine at Rosings for we have received a personal invite every Sunday since my ordination, with the exception of any occasion when we fell out of favour with her ladyship, through no fault of our own. We were so unprepared for such an occurrence, indeed, that we had not appropriate rations of food in the larder, nor staff on duty to prepare it, that we were forced to eat boiled eggs and bread for dinner (as we had for breakfast that morning). I was almost out of my senses with fretting that one of two things had occurred – either some mischief or calamity had befallen her ladyship or we had fallen out of favour yet again without any indication of what which we could be accused of.

I decided to go at once to Rosings, not for to call on her ladyship, but to observe from a distance and reassure myself that nothing of a sinister nature had taken place. If unable to establish this by observation, I would discreetly make enquiries at the servants' quarter. I moved with purpose and was most fortunate that a full moon lit my way but before I approached the lodge house I noticed her ladyship walking in my direction towards the gate. I leapt behind a bush – I know not why I jumped, or what or whom I feared, but that Lady Catherine would be most displeased with me for lurking about at night, I was certain. She stopped at the door of the lodge house and moved no further. I was at a loss as what to do but I was confident that, on such a cold night, she would surely return to the comforts of her home soon.

After several minutes, I saw a figure emerge from the gable end of the house and walk straight up to her ladyship yelling "Where is it?" It was the unmistakeable voice of Smellie but instead of appearing alarmed, her ladyship stepped forward and said in a deep voice, as she raised her arm to strike Smellie, "Never!" A scuffle ensued and before I knew it I was on Smellie's back and being swung around and around until I was finally flung to the ground. As I rose to my feet, I saw Smellie had made good his escape and her ladyship in pursuit with *lifted skirt (pardon my language, sir) but the cumbersomeness of her clothing stifled her progress and she returned to where I was now arising to reveal herself as Giles, Rosings' butler, in disguise.*

I put my fists up and threatened the butler, for I knew not what trickery was underway that had him dressed in her ladyship's clothing and the criminal, Smellie, meeting with him on the grounds of Rosings. Fortunately for him, he spoke up at once, "Fear not, Mr Collins, it is me Giles. Her ladyship had me come here in disguise as a trap for Smellie. It was he who wrote the letters. It is all going to plan. Come back with me to Rosings. It will all be over soon and her ladyship will return."

I cautiously left with him for Rosings but as I felt he might have lost his mind or was not to be trusted, I entered in my usual manner and asked to speak with Lady Catherine on urgent business that could not wait. I was informed she was not at home but was due back shortly, if I cared to wait. To get to the point of the matter, all was explained on her return. Her ladyship had recognised Smellie's handwriting, having several documents about the house which he had written during his stay at Rosings. She was also able to track down how, and from whence, the letters were dispatched which led her to lodgings in Meryton where Smellie was in residence. As Giles met the blackmailer at an agreed time and location to supposedly 'hand over' money, Lady Catherine and some local officers descended upon his lodgings in town and seized a number of stolen artifacts, illegal documentation and evidence of his attempting to extract wealth by blackmail and, as he is still considered a criminal 'on the run', he was arrested immediately on his return (for they were expecting him) and was sent to the barracks at Maidstone.

Thankfully, this is the reason we were not invited to dine on Sunday evening and, if anything, it has cemented our standing and connection with Rosings even further as Lady Catherine confirmed that she is "blessed" with the residents at Hunsford and so, we find, a sense of calm is falling down upon our lives again.

A most wonderful Christmas to all at Longbourn.

Your cousin,

William Collins

Longbourn,
near Meryton,
Hertfordshire.

21st December, 1797

Dear Sir,

A very Merry Christmas to all at Hunsford and Rosings.

What an extraordinary turn of events. That rascal Smellie!
One should send him his own books to read in prison as
punishment for his wicked ways. What a fool to attempt to get
a trick up on her ladyship – he knew not with whom he was
dealing in that instance … a short-cut to his own demise, if
ever there was one.

Yes, Mrs Bennet and I are blessed to have all the girls and
their families about this Christmas and though it be noisy, I
find I can retreat to the solitude of my library and my hearing
impediment takes care of the rest.

Our incredible news, though it hardly competes with a
butler in lady's clothing, is that Mr Luther is now one of the
wealthiest men in Hertfordshire. Apparently his "poisonous"
mixture was in fact an alcoholic spirit of excellent quality,
the recipe for which he has sold for a great fortune to a large
brewing company in Manchester who are readying themselves
for global exportation, even as I write. Perhaps he is now an
acquaintance worth your notice in future and, particularly,
as he has informed the Smocks of his intention of buying
Netherfield Hall if ever they consider quitting it.

I am glad that you may all sleep soundly in your beds now
that Smellie is captured but I do wish the Scots had been let

loose on him first. Again, please extend the fondest sentiments of all at Longbourn to all at Hunsford and Rosings this Christmas and New Year.

Your affectionate cousin,

Henry Bennet

1798 — The year in which we lose a loved one

Longbourn,
near Meryton,
Hertfordshire.

4th January, 1798

Dear Sir,

I hope this letter finds you all well. Pardon me if this letter causes you alarm. I am sure there is nothing to worry about but I feel I should write to my heir on this occasion.

My chest has worsened and all at Longbourn look concerned. The girls have delayed their journeys home which does not bode well, for they have spoken with the physician in secret. This week will tell much so be on your guard, sir, lest you inherit Longbourn before you expect.

I will write again next week when all is returned to normal.
Your cousin,

Henry Bennet

Postscript – I have told dear, distraught Mrs Bennet that Thomas is to have the pigs though it be not yet written in my will.

Longbourn,
near Meryton,
Hertfordshire.

5th January, 1798

Dear Sir,

My last correspondence is incorrect. Come at once, if you please, my heir and friend. The physician looks grave!

    Henry Bennet

Hunsford,
near Westerham,
Kent.

6th January, 1798

Dear Sir,

I depart at once and will not be far behind this express for Lady Catherine has sent her carriage. God grant you solace.
Your affectionate friend and cousin,

William Collins

Hunsford,
near Westerham,
Kent.

1st February, 1798

Dear Mrs Bennet,

Please be assured that your esteemed self, Master Georgie and all your family continue to be included in my daily prayers. I greatly wish there was anything that could be said or written which would bring comfort to you in this time of intense grief and loss other than the certain knowledge that our dear Mr Bennet is most assuredly in the company of our Lord.

Charlotte and Lady Catherine join me in these sentiments and Thomas is particularly glum at present for he has surely lost a true friend and companion.

And though it is a constant and natural function of my sacred vocation to meet others in the valley of the shadow of death, rarely have I felt a loss so keenly. Please forgive me again for weeping so at Mr Bennet's memorial service but he and I not only shared the same bloodline but were altogether as one mind and spirit in so many ways. Our written correspondence, he frequently informed me, furnished him with an enjoyment of life and an understanding of man, which gave life meaning and depth. Indeed, he may rarely have voiced it but I felt the warmth of his affection and esteem at all times and never more so than when, on his deathbed, his parting words to me were that I should read all my great passages at his funeral service, for though he would not be there to hear them, it would give him great comfort and delight to know that his loved ones would.

I continue with great humility and generosity of spirit when I add that although it be a delicate subject, I would like to gently inform you that we have, earlier this week, received a legal letter transferring the entailment of the Longbourn estate to my own name but, please, dear madam, be assured that we are in no hurry to move into Hertfordshire yet. I have been made aware in a letter from my dear cousin Jane that you and Master Georgie are to live with the Bingleys and will be joining them before Easter. Howsoever that may be the case, please know that we will not be leaving Kent until late summer at the earliest, as I have to discover a suitable replacement to execute my duties who will satisfy Lady Catherine's especially high standards.

Let me reassure you once more, Mrs Bennet, that Longbourn will always be your home and I do sincerely hope, as does my dear Charlotte, that you will come stay to with us and visit your many friends and family at Meryton and Lucas Lodge, as well as your dear husband's final resting place, as frequently as you wish.

Know that it is my intention to visit Mr Bennet's grave daily, as I return from church, and to continue to hold counsel with him from beyond the grave, for he was the greatest friend of my life.

"Because he bends down to listen, I will pray as long as I have breath" Psalm 116:2

Your ever humble servant,

William Collins

Afterword

According to census and church records, Mr William Collins went on to live at Longbourn, with his family, until his death on May 12th, 1828. He is buried in the adjoining graveyard, where Mr Henry Bennet is also buried. His eldest son Thomas inherited the Longbourn estate. The current owner, Jane Jenkins, purchased the house and gardens (the agricultural land had been sold in a separate auction) in 2013 and is a direct descendant of the Bennets and Collinses.

Acknowledgements

To my parents and family – if blood is thicker than water, then we are made of mortar. I love you all.

To my friends, dipping in and out of each other's lives – thank you for journeying through life with me and providing fun, support and laughter.

A big thank you to Diarmuid for saying "Just do it!" so I did. To Mags & Shemie for saying they'd give it to me between the eyes, which they did, but kindly so. To Peter and Eileen of the Cork Friends of Jane Austen who were so generous with their time, advice and knowledge, I cannot thank you enough.

To Jane Austen, and all the creative people whom she has inspired through the ages, you have added enormously to this world.

To my greatest blessings, who always believe in me, my nucleus – Filip, Laura and Charlie – such joy!

And, finally, to that love which flows through all things, thank you.